Roses
in
Autumn

Other Five Star Titles
by Donna Fletcher Crow:

Encounter the Light

Roses
in
Autumn

Virtuous Heart Series
Book Two

Donna Fletcher Crow

Five Star • Waterville, Maine

Copyright © 1998
by Beacon Hill Press of Kansas City

All Scripture quotations are from the King James Version
(KJV).

All rights reserved.

Published in 2004 in conjunction with
Beacon Hill Press of Kansas City.

The text of this edition is unabridged.

Set in 11 pt. Plantin by Minnie B. Raven.

Printed in the United States on permanent paper.

Library of Congress Cataloging-in-Publication Data

Crow, Donna Fletcher.
    Roses in autumn / Donna Fletcher Crow.
       p. cm.—(Virtuous heart series ; bk. 2)
    Originally published: Kansas City, Mo. : Beacon Hill
Press of Kansas City, c1998. (Virtuous heart series ; bk. 2).
Includes bibliographical references (p. 224).
    ISBN 1-59414-085-5 (hc : alk. paper)
    1. Intimacy (Psychology)—Religious aspects—
Christianity—Fiction. 2. Marriage—Religious aspects—
Christianity—Fiction. 3. Marriage counseling—Fiction.
 4. Victoria (B.C.)—Fiction. 5. Christian life—Fiction.
I. Title
PS3553.R5872R67 2004

813´.54—dc22   2003049421

The wilderness and the solitary place shall be glad for them;
and the desert shall rejoice, and blossom as the rose.

Isa. 35:1

Introduction

When I was 17 years old, I was in a serious motorcycle accident. As I lay groggily in the emergency room, a nurse leaned over me and told me the doctors would have to cut open my sweatshirt. My immediate thought was, "I'm sure glad I'm wearing clean underwear like my mother always told me."

I didn't give that response much thought until years later when my husband and I started assisting couples one-on-one. I came to a better understanding of the influential impact our parents' attitudes and actions have on each of us and how they build healthy or unhealthy attitudes and actions in *our marriages*.

We have found this especially true in the area of intimacy. If a mother has not had a good sexual relationship with her husband, she may pass that attitude on to her daughter. Her daughter then views sex merely as a duty and not as part of the wonderful gift of marriage given by the Heavenly Father.

We have also discovered many women have been sexually abused when they were children, and their families' response to the abuse situation dramatically affected their view of intimacy and their relationship with their husband.

Instead of sweeping the issue under the carpet, a tool of healing God uses for struggling spouses is Christian counseling. My husband and I have seen when the individual or couple seek help, God often uses counseling to renew a marriage and build it into what He intended it to be.

Donna Fletcher Crow has written an engaging story,

intertwining a couple's struggles and the use of Christian counseling to help restore their marriage. She demystifies the process and shows that at times in our life and marriage, it is appropriate to seek godly, professional help.

As you read this book, may you be entertained, enlightened, and encouraged with the message that God can heal marriages for those who seek Him.

Yvonne Turnbull
Marriage Conference Speaker and Coauthor of *Team-Mates*

Chapter 1

I've never been superstitious, but the night my world shattered was Friday the 13th . . .

That was yesterday. Today Laura James was able to write about it. But then, she was a writer. No, she wasn't superstitious or suspicious. She had never intended to snoop or pry. She never had the slightest suspicion there was anything to snoop or pry about. She was just lonesome and naive.

Tom worked late so many nights. Not to mention the out-of-town traveling his entrepreneurial job required. And the hours of solitude were perfect for the reading and thinking Laura's writing career required. But she wanted her husband's companionship too.

Just this past year his real estate finance business had gone wild. He had overseen developments all over the Northwest and California, and now there was this really big deal in Kansas—the one he had dreamed of for years. People kept asking Tom and his partner, Phil, if they would be moving. But when you were as spread out as that, there was no one place to move to, and as long as planes kept flying into and out of Boise, it was as good a place to live as any.

But Tom and Laura were apart so much. Sometimes she missed the good old days when there wasn't enough work or enough money but plenty of time.

Well, it was only eleven o'clock. She would fill a basket with goodies and surprise him with a midnight picnic at the office.

Laura washed a cluster of pale green grapes, at their September sweetest, then put a wedge of creamy Port du Salut cheese in the basket—just for Tom—next to her slice of fat-free cheddar. Smiling, she thought how surprised Tom would be and how they would laugh, sitting together on the office floor. She took a package of éclairs out of the freezer to add to her trove. Maybe she would even eat one tonight. When the teakettle whistled, she filled the Thermos with Almond Pleasure tea, and her work was done. All that remained was to brush her short, curly, nut-brown hair and slip on a crisp shirt over her tailored skirt.

The night air was still warm and languid. As she walked from her little car to the black marble-fronted office building, she felt the heat of the day emanating from the cement sidewalk while hints of the coming autumn crispness lurked in the air. But in the building's small foyer, the air-conditioning returned the atmosphere to its seasonless comfort. Laura inserted her key in the elevator and pushed the button for the third floor.

When she stepped off the elevator, all was dark and quiet in the reception room of Marsden and James, Inc., but she could see a slim strip of light under Tom's door. The tweed carpet muffled every sound as she crossed to his office and flung the door open wide.

"Surprise, Darling!"

She stood encased in timeless, disbelieving horror. What were these people doing in Tom's office? Even when he had disentangled himself from the woman's embrace, Laura still couldn't accept that it was Tom. It was as if some strange man was holding a woman in Tom's office.

Part of her muddled brain wanted to say, "Excuse me, but where's Tom?" while another part of it wanted to scream and claw and throw things. But she didn't do anything.

She didn't know how long she would have stood there, mute and immobile while her brain lurched and shrieked, if Tom hadn't moved. He took two steps toward her. "Laura, I believe you know Marla Kauffman, the real estate agent I've been working with."

"Hello . . ." She actually started to acknowledge the introduction as if at a formal reception. Then the frozen horror melted and flooded her. She turned and ran from the building, taking the stairs because waiting for an elevator was unthinkable.

At home, her favorite wingback chair received her like a mother's arms, and she sat there in blindness, silent tears flowing down her cheeks. A long time later she heard Tom's car on the driveway, then his key in the lock. She made no motion to respond.

"Laura, I'm so sorry."

A small corner somewhere in Laura's brain registered that Tom looked as if he'd aged 10 years.

"I wouldn't hurt you for the world. I don't even know how it happened." He sank heavily onto the bench at the foot of the bed—their bed—where they had slept together for seven years.

"Not hurt me?" She sprang at him. A blaze of anger burned her tears away. "*Not hurt me!* You thought you could carry on with another woman and 'not hurt me'?" Was he that stupid, or did he think she was? "You never thought of whether or not you'd hurt me. You just thought I wouldn't find out! If you thought at all!"

His shoulders slumped. "Laura, I . . ."

"Oh, don't try to explain. For God's sake, don't make excuses."

The shock on his face was indescribable.

"Oh, don't worry. I wasn't swearing. I was praying. You

may have thrown everything you believe into the wind for the sake of a fling, but I haven't."

. . . It was as I said it that I understood. I was able to put the awful, gaping wound inside me into words. I hadn't made Tom my god—but I realized then that my faith in him had been as complete. As unshakable. I sank back into my chair, all anger gone. In slow, hollow tones I said, "It's as if God were dead."

Laura closed her journal. Reliving last night's scenes had been almost as painful as the initial experience. But now her mind was clear. It was a catharsis. Getting it on paper got it out of her head. Now she could think about something else.

She sat there for some time, biting one fingernail, seeing Tom's face as she spoke those words. If she had been trying to hurt him—seeking revenge—she could have done nothing more effective. He sat for several minutes, his head bent forward as if he had received a physical blow. Then he got up slowly and went to the guestroom.

It was nearly noon the next day—today, that was—but Laura's grasp on time was tenuous and slippery. They met in the kitchen. The teakettle was singing, the sun shining on a glossy Swedish ivy hanging by the window, and the red and white silk-screened wallpaper looking as vibrant as ever. But to Laura the world was a dull gray. As she poured the bubbling water over the English Breakfast tea leaves, she noted that in spite of his taking care to shave and brush his smooth blond hair into place, Tom looked as war-ravaged as she felt.

Mechanically she put two slices of honey wheat bread in the toaster and waited for them to pop up. It wasn't until they were sitting in their usual places at the glass-topped white wrought iron table that Tom broke the silence. "Laura," his voice was husky, almost pleading. "What do you want to do now?"

She shook her head, deliberately poured skim milk into

her tea, and took a long sip before she answered. "What I want is for it never to have happened. But since it did, I suppose you'd better tell me about it." She held her teacup with both hands and stared at it. She knew Tom wasn't looking at her either.

"There's so little to tell. Marla's agency had some finance questions we couldn't answer about the Kansas project. So we've been working for days—weeks, I guess—on computer runs to see what happens to the profits if the builder is his own investor—things like that. Last night we were finally getting the answers. And they were good—incredibly good—beyond our wildest expectations. And then we were hugging each other . . ."

"You expect me to believe that? That all I saw was a joy of the moment celebration of a good computer run?" Her cup landed in her saucer with an angry crash.

Tom shook his head and looked at her with dead eyes. "No. I'm not trying to soft-pedal it. I'm just trying to explain what happened."

"So there was more? How much more?" She probed with the ruthlessness of a surgeon excising a cancer. She didn't want to know. She didn't want there to be anything to know. But her life depended on finding the truth.

His voice was as lifeless as his eyes. "I don't know."

"You don't know? You mean you've been cuddling her so much you lost count?"

"No!" Tom came off his chair and leaned across the table toward Laura. "No. That was the first time—and the last. What you saw was all there was. I hugged her. We had all our clothes on, for goodness' sake."

Laura waited. Tom took his seat. He sighed and ran his fingers through his hair, rumpling its silken smoothness. "I don't even remember the first time we met. Some meeting with some potential investor. Who knows? But when we started focusing on this project we discovered we read all the same columnists in the *Wall Street Journal* and *The Economist*. Somewhere along the way we discovered we both prefer Sumatra Roast . . ."

Laura looked at the splattered remains of her tea. She hated coffee.

". . . and Gershwin . . ."

Laura moved to snap off her Mozart CD, then realized she hadn't started it.

". . . I'd get an idea about the project and couldn't wait to tell her about it . . ."

"And you assumed I wouldn't be interested—or wouldn't understand."

"Well, investment formulas have never been your favorite topic of conversation."

"And so, last night . . ." Laura prompted him back to the subject at hand. They weren't discussing her shortcomings at the moment.

Tom shook his head. "It started as simple celebration. But—she felt so good in my arms—so warm and responsive. Before God, I'm sorry, Laura. But the least I can do is be honest with you. If you hadn't come in . . . Laura, you've got to believe how very, very thankful I am that you *did* come in. But I can't honestly say what might have happened . . . God help me." He put his head down, supporting it with one hand. "I don't know. I just don't know."

Hundreds of unformed questions whirled in Laura's mind. After a time she was able to grab one of them. "Did you feel guilty?"

"There was nothing to feel guilty about! We never kissed. Never held hands. Not even one time. I told you."

Laura was surprised at the note of grimness in his voice—

as if it had required a great deal of self-control that the case should be so. She tried to remember. She had met the woman on a few occasions. Marla wasn't beautiful, but her long strawberry blond hair and porcelain skin gave her a look of fragility that was undeniably appealing. And she had long, slim legs that Laura had more than once eyed with envy, since she always wore ankle-length skirts to cover her own less attractive legs.

She looked at Tom, remembering. Then she knew what had hurt her most last night. Her voice was barely above a whisper. "You looked at her the way you used to look at me."

Silence pressed the ceiling lower and lower while remembered words and scenes ricocheted off the walls, more piercing than bullets. For a moment the vision of Marla's arms around Tom's neck was so vivid she thought she was going to be sick.

Suddenly she was on her feet, screaming at him. "It's—it's horrible! Disgusting! How could you? Like some depraved animal!"

"Well, now. That's more like it. About time we got around to that, isn't it?" Tom slammed his fist on the table, making the glass rattle. Any suggestion of groveling vanished. "Right! Let's talk about *your* hang-ups now. It took two to make this mess, you know!"

"It certainly did take two. It took you and Marla!" Tears stung the backs of her eyes, but she fought them away fiercely and kept them down with her anger.

Anger was her only defense against Tom's challenge. "Marla's only a symptom, and you know it. We're going to talk about us. A talk we should have had seven years ago."

"You can't blame me for your—your philandering!"

"I take full responsibility for last night. And I intend to take full responsibility for my future. And if you can't treat my love for you as something other than depraved and animal, I'll find someone who will. So help me."

"Love! What you're talking about isn't love. It's lust! And you know perfectly well I've never denied you your rights. Never. Not once in seven years."

"Oh, no. You've been the perfect, submissive wife. But you've never accepted my lovemaking as anything more than a duty. How do you think that makes me feel? It so happens I'm a human being with feelings, and I would like to feel that my wife takes pleasure in my company in bed. You've never shown the least response in our whole married life."

"And it therefore follows that you've never had pleasure in my company in all this time?" Her throat was so tight she was surprised her voice could come out.

"Your logic is impeccable. Just like the rest of you— impeccable, perfect, and passionless!"

It wasn't until she heard his engine roar in the driveway that she realized he had left the house. Had he gone to the office? Of course. What else? Would Marla be there?

Laura wanted to scream, hit, tear something. If Tom hadn't left, she would have lashed at him with her bitten fingernails. She wanted to wound him as she was wounded. She sat there, replaying scene after scene in her mind. Last night in the office—if only she had flung the picnic basket at them. Or better yet, the contents one at a time . . . She smiled at the thought of that silky strawberry hair with chocolate éclairs rubbed in it, the soft crepe blouse drenched in Almond Pleasure tea . . .

Or sneak up behind them still locked in their embrace and pour the steaming contents of the Thermos over their heads. If Tom wanted a steamy romance, she'd give him one. And then scream at him. Smash his precious computer. Shred his exalted spreadsheets with those tidy columns of figures . . .

She sighed. Of course she would do no such thing, but living it out in her head was cathartic. Laura stumbled down the hall and sought refuge again in her favorite chair.

Still unable to face the present, she turned her thoughts from the past to the future. And again she faced the empty "God is dead" void. How could she bear it? Could she ever trust Tom again? Could she ever stand to let him touch her now? If he ever took her in his arms again, would he be thinking of Marla? Would *she* be thinking of Marla? Would that other woman always be there between them?

And yet, what if he never held her again? Last night with him in the next room had been unbearable. She had become accustomed to his absence on business trips, but to have him sleep in another bed when he was home was unthinkable.

Bed. She thought of the warm comfort of him curled beside her. Then her senses revolted and she could think no further.

Chapter 2

Tom was home for dinner at his usual hour. And Laura had done dishes and laundry and scrubbed the bathroom and spent two hours at her computer, as if it had been any other day. Strange; the world could be ravaged by war or earthquake or infidelity, yet the daily pattern continued. People needed food and clothing and shelter, and it was a woman's job to provide it. Old-fashioned thinking, maybe, but the way the world worked. In normal times it was a woman's burden, but in a time of crisis it could also be her salvation. Take refuge in the routine, the small, the nitty-gritty details that keep the world turning. Even when there is no world left to turn.

"How was your day?" Anything to break the silence. It was the first time in seven years she hadn't met him at the door with a kiss. They both seemed at a loss without it.

"Busy. I approved the advertising campaign for the condos in Palm Desert. Then Phil and I went over the proposed contracts before we negotiate the K.C. deal."

It didn't *sound* like he'd been with Marla. "Oh, is Philip back?" Philip Marsden, Tom's partner, was the legal brain while Tom was the marketing expert. They made a powerful team. But Phil was older and not in good health. He was considerably past retirement age, but his creative, energetic mind wouldn't retire, even if his body and his wife wanted him to.

"He claims the week in Sun Valley rested him completely. But I suspect he worked every minute Lois turned her back." Tom set down his briefcase and pulled off his jacket.

It was so easy. It was almost as if the past 18 hours hadn't happened. Laura turned to slice mushrooms for their green salad while Tom put on tall glasses of ice water. The crazy idea came to her that they could simply go on from here. She could pretend it was all something she had read in a book—in a florid, poorly written romance—something that had nothing to do with her or with real life.

She set the bowls of stroganoff and noodles on the table. Tom held her chair for her as he always did. They bowed their heads for a brief grace. Laura took a bite of bread—and choked. It simply would not go down. The little ball of dough stuck in her throat. There was nothing to do but go to the sink.

The rest of the evening was a disaster. The green salad wilted and the untouched stroganoff congealed in its sour cream sauce while they alternately flung threats and recriminations at each other, rehashing everything they had said that morning—only saying it with greater violence each time around.

It was sheer exhaustion that finally brought it to a stop. "I'm going to pack now." Tom wrenched open his closet door. "I leave for Kansas City in the morning. I'll stay at the airport hotel for what's left of tonight. I can't face those high-powered syndicators tomorrow without any sleep." He began stuffing shirts and ties into the carry-on bag he always used for business trips.

On his second time out of the bathroom with toothpaste tube and red toothbrush still in his hand, Laura found the courage to ask, "And when will you be back?"

"What makes you think I'm coming back?" He crammed the zipper shut on his case and flung himself out the door.

The next four days Laura spent in a state of suspended animation. She thought of calling her mother in Texas but couldn't bear the thought of hearing that tight, accusing voice telling her it was all her fault. She thought of calling their pastor, but she didn't just want a shoulder to cry on; and she knew any serious counseling would have to be a joint effort. She thought of reading her Bible and praying . . . but God was dead. When there was no one to pray to, there were no answers.

She tried to write, but her heroine's problems were insipid and contrived next to her own. Her journal was her only solace. She wrote until the words ran out and the blank pages jeered at her. She put the cap on her pen and began looking back through the pages of her life—not reading the words but reliving the scenes:

A debate tournament at some college in southern Oregon. ". . . and this is Tom James, the Great White Hope of Rocky Mountain's debate squad." Instant friendship between our teams because we were from sister colleges, established by the same denomination. Later that day, dragging back to the central lounge, exhausted after a grueling round of debate. Tom waved to me from across the room crowded and noisy with faceless bodies. I wasn't tired anymore.

Double date that night. Tom with my debate partner and I with his. Got it right later. Transferred to Rocky Mountain College at semester. A debate romance; a wonderful time together on every trip the team took, then something always went wrong—usually my fault—and we'd not speak to each other back on campus.

And then that tournament in North Dakota—at a Black Hills resort, of all places. A long walk down a dusty country lane the first evening. Tom's arm around my shoulders in the cool air. The sunset a pale yellow in a pastel blue sky behind a newly green field. Went back to my room and pounded the saggy iron bed with my fists because I was in love, and I had blown so many chances with Tom. Nobody got that many second chances. But I did. For years we celebrated the sixth of every month because we had fallen in love on April 6.

Tom.

A perfect June wedding with my bridesmaids in long yellow dresses and picture hats. Our reception on the church lawn. Afterward, I saw the photograph of my bridesmaids on the grass and realized they looked like daffodils in the breeze. But that afternoon I had eyes only for Tom, stunning with his boyish smile and tender eyes, his tall, lean grace and thick blond hair, his tuxedo and ruffled shirt. "To love, honor, and cherish till death do us part." The Lord's Prayer on the violin while we knelt and took Communion to symbolize the Lord's presence at our wedding and in our lives.

Our honeymoon to Carmel-by-the-Sea. Wandered through tiny streets, browsed in art shops, ate ice-cream cones at a sidewalk café, took pictures of each other under the gnarled old cypress tree on the beach. Then romped in the glorious white sand and blue surf, shared an unspeakable spiritual closeness when we prayed together, awoke in the middle of the night to find Tom raised on one elbow beside me, stroking me with gentle wonder. Inexpressible tenderness.

Tom.

That wonderful lazy summer in our tiny apartment. Midnight rambles along the greenbelt, then sleeping till noon because Tom's job in the grocery store didn't start until 1:30. The fun it was to waken first, slip out, and fix breakfast so I could surprise Tom with a tray in bed. Everything so idyllic. Perfect, really. All except one thing. And Tom was patient and loving about that.

Tom.

Then packing to move East where we both had scholarships for graduate school. Hearing the tornado warnings on the radio as we crossed into western Nebraska. Feeling tense all the way across the state because all our earthly possessions are in that little U-Haul trailer. Tom studying for his Harvard M.B.A. Me sitting beside him reading for my English degree from Boston University. Reveling in the student life in those sleek, high-rise apartments along the Charles River. Walking through piles of rustling leaves to Harvard Square. Driving along country lanes under breath-taking fall foliage. Stopping at little roadside stands to buy jam and apples from children.

Snow. I had never seen such snow. My first blizzard. The Charles froze, and Tom and his classmates walked across the ice to the Business School. A weekend at the picture calendar village of Newfane, reading art books by a roaring fire in the inn, then going to our room furnished with genuine antiques. And still Tom was understanding.

Tom.

Spring in New England. Coming late, so appreciated more. Walking hand-in-hand through the sweet, green countryside. Watching the fish jump in Walden Pond.

Oh, Tom. How can I live without you?

Moving to Boise where Tom had a job with M-K. All his class-mates going to Wall Street or Chicago or Philadelphia. But we wanted to live in the West—a smaller city was better for raising a family.

Oh, Tom. I failed you again.

Being busy and happy. Really happy. Fixing up our new home—well, actually 72 years old, but new to us; getting involved at church. Tom surprising me by volunteering to teach a class of nine-year-old boys. Building our careers: me writing for every opportunity that appeared—poetry, curriculum, devotionals— Tom working day and night to meet the challenges of corporate America. Tom, the poor son of an alcoholic father, so determined to make good and always working for the extra bonus so he could send something to his mother and younger sister in Portland.

Then the frustration. Tom, still driven for the money he had never had, but bored with his work because he had met and con-

quered all the challenges his corporate pigeonhole offered. The rejections coming back faster than I could mail out manuscripts. And every month my body telling me I'd failed there too. Filling the extra time with more church work. Tom took on a Scout troop. I took on the drama ministry. And still we had time. Time for bike rides together along Boise's quiet old tree-lined North End streets. Time for weekend trips to the mountains. Time to make homemade ice cream. Time to be with Tom.

Tom.

The seemingly overnight change. Tom's brainchild—a system for people to buy new homes without a down payment. "It will make the American dream a possibility to thousands who never had a chance!" Tom as excited as he used to be when he came up with a particularly ingenious debate plan. And my form rejection letters changed to personal letters: "Sorry, this doesn't fit our line, but why don't you try . . ." And then an acceptance! Three contracts in one spring.

Everything perfect. Everything but one. And Tom was becoming less patient.

And now. All that success and happiness had led to this. But it wasn't the fault of the success and happiness. It was Tom's fault. Wasn't it? Tom implied it was partly my fault. I suppose it takes two, that's what Tom said. Sometimes I think it's God's fault. Why did He have to create men to be such animals? Tom was so perfect in every other way.

Oh, Tom. Tom.

Laura's face and journal were both wet. But all that reminiscing, walking again through the pages of their lives, had made one thing absolutely clear in her mind and in her heart. She wanted Tom. More than anything else in the world, she wanted Tom. And she would do anything to get him back.

She didn't have any idea what she could do, but knowing what she wanted ignited a clear, shining light that burned through her gray haze—a beacon to follow. And Tom would be at the end.

The next day two things happened. She received a letter from her agent. And Tom came back.

"Well . . ." He cleared his throat.

She was sitting at her computer in the small room that opened off the master bedroom through French doors, and she hadn't heard him come in. She must have jumped three inches off her chair at the sound of his voice. It made her feel a fool. "Oh, Tom, I . . ." She sprang up to meet him with delight shining from her face. But she stopped cold at the solid wall his countenance presented. "You're back," she finished weakly.

"You may recall I only packed enough clothes for the trip." His voice was as hard as his features.

She stood blinking dumbly as he turned to his closet. No, wait! This wasn't right. It wasn't supposed to happen this way. She had decided they would go on. They would make it. Everything would be all right.

She was gripped with paralysis as she watched him in seeming slow motion empty the contents of his dresser into two large cardboard boxes. She had to stop this. But it was like a nightmare where she tried and tried to run, but no matter how hard she worked she couldn't make her legs move.

He carried a load of suits and coats to the car and returned for his shirts when she finally found her voice. "Tom, please. Don't do this. Let us *try*." He pulled his hand back from the row of shirts in his closet. Now she was fully awake; she could function. She could fight for her life.

"Tom, I've done so much thinking—all the time you've been gone." She moved a few steps toward him into the bedroom. "Don't go." She held out her hands in pleading. "I love you." There was nothing more to say. Her eyes would have to say the rest for her—her eyes and her heart, which was in her throat.

The deep lines in his face seemed to soften ever so slightly. "What do you want to do?" It was a cautious question with no commitment, but it held out hope. It gave her courage to go on.

"I got a letter from my agent today. And a contract. Cathedral Press liked my proposal. They want to publish *Roses for the Bride.* That means I have to go to Victoria for background research." She paused and took a deep breath to give her courage for the next part. "Come with me."

Her whole life had passed before her when she reread her journal. It did a quick rerun now as she awaited Tom's answer.

"I'll think about it." He walked from the room, leaving his shirts in the closet.

Chapter 3

There are no airsick bags on this plane! Between the lurches and drops of the little San Juan commuter plane, Laura hunted frantically in the seat-back pouches around her—but to no avail. *What am I going to do?* Strong winds buffeted the small propjet making its last flight of the night across the Strait of Juan de Fuca from Seattle to Vancouver Island while Laura, with one hand over her mouth, looked around desperately.

Tom sat stoically beside her, his eyes focused on the sharp crease of his dark blue suit pants. *He'll kill me if I get sick on him. And this was supposed to be a honeymoon.*

She clamped her hand tighter, her thumb against her nose to keep out the stench of stale cigar smoke clinging to a nearby passenger. They were so compactly sardined in the narrow seats that every blast of wind threw her against the passenger across the so-called aisle and then bounced her off Tom's shoulder. "You'll have a wonderful time!" their neighbor had said over and over. If only she could see her now. And Tom, whom she longed so to reach, seemed stiffer and more remote each time she lunged into him. *This is going to be the shortest reconciliation on record.*

What am I going to do? Feeling too awful even to breathe, let alone think, Laura found the answer. She pulled the safety information card and airline magazine from the pocket in front of her and put her head down. The clean-up crew would earn their keep tonight.

"Well, folks, here we are. That was a little bumpy, wasn't

it? Sorry if any of you felt any discomfort. We were delayed getting out of Seattle, so it's getting pretty late here, but thank you for flying San Juan." The pilot, grinning from ear to ear, emerged from the curtained cockpit to dismiss his load of sardines to the mercies of the black, rain-drenched, wind-whipped night.

Tom pulled Laura's case from the overhead bin behind them and supported her off the plane into the tiny, almost deserted airport for the customs formalities conducted by officials who couldn't talk about anything but the unseasonableness of the storm. The bright lights made Laura blink. "Don't look at me, Tom. I look awful in pea green."

There were no porters available, so while Tom signed the rental car papers handed him by a yawning girl behind a counter, Laura struggled with their luggage at the carousel. "Let me help you with those, ma'am."

Laura gave a weak but grateful smile to the tall, broad man with curly dark hair beside her.

"Thank you. The big blue one just coming up now . . . and the little one over there . . . and the black—"

"I'll take care of that. Thanks anyway." Tom stepped in front of the helpful stranger and began jerking bags off the carousel. "Come on, Laura. If I get these, can you handle those three?" Laura had packed generously for their two weeks, but even then she hadn't realized she had brought quite so much.

"Why don't you take those to the car, and I'll stay here with the others?"

"We can make it all in one trip. I don't want to leave you here alone for one of those French-Canadian mashers."

Laura had a fleeting sensation that she ought to be flattered that he cared, but at the moment just carrying her assigned bags took all her concentration. Crossing the street to the parking lot, a fresh blast of wind practically blew her over. "Steady on," Tom encouraged her.

Steady. She repeated the word over and over to herself to the rhythm of the windshield wipers as their little white rental car swished bravely through the downpour. Her head felt wobbly on her neck, her knees were as supportive as sprung Slinkies, and her stomach didn't bear thinking of at all. "I didn't know the island was this big." *Keep your mind off yourself.*

"The airport's at the far end. We'll soon be there."

"You're sure you know the way?"

"No problem. There's only one way."

Laura would have liked to pursue the thought that life should be so simple. But at the moment, she wanted even more not to think at all.

"See? The lights of the city. What'd I tell you?" Even in her near-comatose state Laura admired her husband's ability to find his way in a strange city in the black of night. Laura had a mind that could memorize poetry at little more than a single reading, but she couldn't remember directions or a math formula to save herself from hanging. Tom whipped around three corners, and there before her appeared the fairy-tale scene of the many-domed Parliament building all outlined in lights. She had seen the pictures but assumed the illumination was only done at Christmas. And now, after all the time she had dreamed of seeing it, here she was—too wretched to care. Tom turned up a dim, rain-washed driveway and stopped under the portals of the Empress Hotel.

But grande dame that she was, the Empress needed her sleep. And apparently so did her doorman and bellman. So Laura made her entrance into one of the world's great hotels tripping over bulging bags and struggling to see around the straggles of wet hair hanging over her eyes. So much for all of her daydreams of the beautiful, romantic times they would have in the garden city of the world—how they would redis-cover each other and learn to love in a whole new way, the honeymoon that would be a prelude to the rest of their lives . . . She had undoubtedly endued the venture with too much fantasy—that was typical of her—but she could never have imagined this reality.

Consciousness came slowly the next morning as Laura lay looking up at the jade green canopy patterned with peach flowers, then snuggled deeper in the comfort of the carved mahogany four-poster that filled the bedroom of their suite.

Tom's breathing was still sleep-heavy on the other side of the big bed. Early rays of gold coming in the high windows told Laura the storm had blown itself out, leaving the promise of a more hospitable first day in Victoria than their inauspi-cious welcome seemed to presage. Moving carefully so as not to awaken Tom, she reached for her journal on the bedside table but knocked the slim pen to the floor. She scrambled to pick it up. Such a nuisance to not have fingernails. She hoisted herself to a semisitting position and began chewing thoughtfully on the end of her pen:

I'm so thankful Tom agreed to come with me—it's so good to have him here in bed beside me. I was afraid he'd book a room with twin beds—or even two rooms—the fact that we're together in this gorgeous antique bed in this lovely old hotel in this romantic city must be a good sign.

She looked at the tousled head of her sleeping husband.

It has to be a good sign. I can't imagine life without him. What would I do? Just the question panics me. But can I possibly hold him? Make him happy? Make him want to stay with me?

Dear God, in our years of marriage I've never really been all I should be. Can I possibly now? Is desperation enough? Help me.

Tom rolled over and stretched lazily. "I'm hungry."

"At least 60 percent stomach." Laura grinned and scooted out of bed to get dressed. She had spent so many years perfecting the switch from her own forlorn longings to the bantering relationship that held their marriage together that she did it now without thinking.

When they stepped off the elevator it was evident that after last night's inhospitality the Empress had returned to her gracious, refined self. The tartan-jacketed gentleman at the carved oak, marble-topped counter pointed across the red-carpeted length of the ivory-pillared lobby filled with Queen Anne furniture. "Down the stairs. Turn right to the Garden Café." It was much more like being in a stately English mansion than the main lobby of a hotel. Except Tom wouldn't have been able to buy a *Wall Street Journal* in a stately home.

They followed the man's directions to a room circled with rose-patterned drapes looped between Corinthian pillars. Pedestaled urns of flowers sitting atop balustrades separated the tables, giving one the feeling of having just stepped through French windows onto the terrace of a Georgian mansion.

Laura asked the waitress for skimmed milk for her tea, then between sips looked over her notes. "Let's do the provincial museum this morning and then have tea at the Crystal Garden. Then we can go to the castle if there's time." A good night of sleep had restored her usual enthusiasm, and the hot milky drink was stirring her energy.

Tom looked up from the *Wall Street Journal* folded discreetly beside his plate. When the waitress brought his platter of bacon and eggs, Laura asked about their house tea. "It's called Empress blend. Murchie's makes it for us." Laura's nod was a mental ticking of her list—Murchie's was on her agenda. She liked having her lists organized. Being the fuzzy,

30

right-brained person she was, lists were her lifeline.

Laura came back from her introspection to pick the raisins from her bran flakes before adding skim milk. Then she looked at Tom. He was chewing a sausage, but his mind was obviously in Sacramento or Kansas City or . . . She shrugged; wherever he was, she wasn't with him. How could she reach him? She looked around for a topic of conversation and sighted two little gray-haired ladies seated across the room. "Look, Tom. They're just like the 'dollar ladies.' "

He didn't exactly frown as he looked up. "Dollar ladies? Sounds sleazy."

She tried not to bristle at his finding an innuendo in her words. He certainly knew her better than that. "Hardly. They were residents of the Empress in the '20s. Elderly ladies living on fat trust accounts—until the stock market crash wiped them out. They had no place to go, so the hotel allowed them to move up to the garret rooms for a dollar a day." Laura strained to keep the conversation light, impersonal.

And her story was rewarded by Tom's warm smile. The smile that in all the time she had known him had never once failed to make her heart turn over. "I like that—the grand hotel with a heart."

Encouraged, she continued, "There are lots of stories about the Empress dowagers." She searched her mind for snatches of her research. "Like when they could no longer afford to eat in the dining room, so they smuggled hot plates into their attic rooms. The management discreetly looked the other way except in the most flagrant cases—like the one who let her homemade strawberry jam boil over, or the one who had to be asked not to cook liver and onions in her room, or another whose penchant for pickling onions had to be restrained."

A small thing, but all at once they were laughing together

over such goings on by dignified little old ladies in the stately halls of the Empress. It was so good to be laughing with Tom again. How long had it been? Weeks? Months, at least. A lifetime? She couldn't really remember. But it meant there was hope. Please, God, it *had* to mean that.

Then she noticed the family seated on the other side of the balustrade from them. "See, my egg melted." The dad pointed to his empty, half eggshell in its tall crystal eggcup. His small son clapped his hands and giggled. Laura looked at Tom just in time to catch his glance at the father and son—and to see the hurt look in his eyes. Again she felt the guilty stab of failure.

"Right. Museum first, then?" Laura was grateful to Tom for breaking the small tension that crept back so quickly.

"It seems a good place to start. I don't suppose Gwendolyn and Kevin would actually go there since they live here, but I need to know some local history for background."

"Gwendolyn and Kevin?"

"My hero and heroine."

"Oh. Yeah. What's your story about?"

"Well, all I've done so far is the first chapter and an outline, but Kevin is a doctor, and he won't make a commitment to Gwen until he can really give their relationship the attention it needs—which he can't do right now because of the demands of his job and some family problems."

"So why does it have to be set in Victoria?"

"Because they live here, silly."

"Uh-ho. Breathing already, are they?"

"Starting to. But I originally chose Victoria because it's such a romantic spot. And because I wanted to do something about rose growing—so what better place than the Butchart Gardens?"

"Well, I wish them happiness."

"Me too, but not too soon." Laura gathered her notes. "I'm not into writing short stories."

"I suppose you'll want to stop at a bookstore first."

"Ah, you know my methods. Guidebooks, maps, local flora and fauna . . ."

"Fine." Tom signaled the waitress for their check. "You go on to your bookstore. I need to go back to the room to make some calls. We've got to firm our offer for the Kansas City deal. This is too good a thing to let go too cheap. I'm going to press for half a point more."

He went on explaining, but Laura wasn't listening. Who was *we?* Marsden and James or Tom and Marla? Her mind spun. Tom was still doing *business?* This was a honeymoon. He was supposed to be here for her. Of course, it was a business trip for her—but that was different.

All the way up the street to the bookstore Laura kept telling herself Tom was just being efficient. After all, his business didn't stop just because he was out of town. And she didn't expect him to follow her around like a puppy dog all the time they were here. After all, if they'd gone to an investment seminar, she wouldn't have attended classes with him. But this wasn't an investment seminar. It was a honeymoon. Wasn't it?

They couldn't build bridges to each other if they weren't together. And Tom had gone off as if he didn't really care—as if he were relieved to be going to work. *No! I won't think like that. If he didn't care at all, he wouldn't have agreed to come with me in the first place . . . Now, you're here to do a job. So do it.*

Laura forced herself to focus on the city around her rather than on her own inner turmoil. By the time she had walked the five blocks from the hotel to the bookstore, admiring the imported tweeds and plaids in the windows, quickly scanning the sumptuous China shops, feeling the almost-warmth of the almost-shining sun on her head, she had become Gwendolyn.

She paused to jot a few notes and stuff them in the brief-case that was always an extension of her arm on a research trip. Then she walked faster to make up for lost time. When she began to feel the bounce in her step, she recalled her ear-lier apprehensions—fear that is always part of the process of writing a novel—the "what if no words come" syndrome. Now with every word that appeared on the notepad she relaxed.

Sometime later she left the bookstore with a heavy package that made her think perhaps her order of activities lacked logic. She dithered: The way to the museum passed the hotel, she could just run the books up to the room. If Tom was already at the museum, though, she didn't want to make him wait. In the end she shifted her parcel to the other arm and hurried on. She looked briefly at the Classic Car museum. Tom would enjoy that, but it wasn't a place Gwendolyn would go. Laura could see that her two lives were going to have to make some compromises.

A shadow fell across her path. She had a sense of someone reaching for her arm. "Tom! How did—?" She turned, but no one was there. Laura smiled and shook her head. Writer's imagination. It could make one feel so foolish sometimes.

She hurried on past the park filled with totem poles—interesting, but not really her thing. And yet, she sensed already that that was one of the charms of Victoria: Olde En-gland alongside Eskimos; Queen Victoria serving tea to Mounties and fur trappers; union jacks and maple leaves. And as if in reply to her musings on cultural mix she nodded to a pole bearing bilingual street signs and a Think Metric mileage marker, giving kilos in white and miles in yellow.

Just finding the main entrance to the enormous, multilevel

provincial museum was something of an accomplishment. And then, how to find the rooms she wanted? And most importantly, where would Tom be? "Where are the period rooms?" She approached a guard.

"Third floor, up the escalator, turn right."

"Thank you." Laura looked around, still feeling dazed at the every-which-way spaces surrounding her. "Do you ever lose people in here?"

"The odd one."

"That'll be me."

"Not to worry. We always find them at 5:30."

Laura smiled and turned toward the escalator, shifting her briefcase and books. She hadn't realized it all weighed so much, but she would just have to get used to it.

"—and then the bit I like best I find when I've got 10 minutes to catch my bus." The lady behind her on the escalator seemed to open a conversation in the middle of a sentence.

"Oh, yes, isn't life like that." Laura smiled, but her mind was on finding Tom. She had told him she wanted to see the period rooms first because a member of her writers' group had recommended them. But would he remember? Should she wait here or go on in? Was he already inside waiting for her? Or was he still on the phone? On the phone with Marla? Well, she certainly wasn't going to stand around here all morning while he chatted up his paramour.

She strode forward and stepped backward 90 years in history: past an old theatre playing a flickering silent movie on the screen, past the city garage housing a flivver named Elizabeth, past the Columbia Printers displaying a window banner announcing Gold in Yukon. At each building her pen moved across the notepad, but her eyes were searching every man that entered. Where was Tom? How would he ever catch up with her in this maze? Why hadn't she made more explicit arrangements? And her book purchases were getting heavier. At least she had a shoulder strap for her briefcase. Thank goodness it was soft-sided, lightweight nylon. Even though it somehow felt about a pound heavier today.

She smiled as she heard a solid, male footstep behind her. "There you are!" She turned, then frowned. No one. And yet she was sure she had heard . . . Oh, well.

She walked on, past the Dominion Drapers displaying elegant Edwardian dresses, Chinese fans, and embroidered satin shoes. Then farther up the street she stepped across the boardwalk into the plush-carpeted Grand Hotel and climbed the wide staircase. Grateful that this was a hands-on museum, she sank onto the red velvet Victorian loveseat on the landing and dropped her books before continuing her note-taking. Coveting the sculptured decoration around the foyer ceiling for her own living room, she sought the right word. "What do you call that trim at the top of the paper?" she asked a fellow visitor, an older lady wearing two antique brooches at her neck.

"Borrder. Joost a borrder."

"Oh."

"It isn't done now."

"No, that's why I like it so much."

"I'm old enough to remember much of it in my grandmother's house—but that was in Scotland." The lady pronounced her homeland's name with a long *o*.

Laura's informant moved on, and she wrote fast to capture the woman on paper, but her pen bogged down. That was the only trouble with a soft briefcase—it didn't make a good writing table. She ran her fingers absently over the slick, padded surface.

"Doesn't that lady look lifelike?" A pair of visitors grinned at her.

"Oh, yes." Laura smiled back. "Part of the display—but I'm afraid I don't look sufficiently Victorian." Everyone here was so friendly and helpful. It seemed Victoria's residents took a personal responsibility to offer friendship and welcome to their tourist guests.

Leaving the town display, Laura walked into a farmyard and stood for several seconds in front of a horse, expecting him to move his head and scare away the chirping birds. Oh, where was Tom? She wanted to share all this with him. They could be having so much fun experiencing it together. Of course, if it didn't work—if they couldn't stick the pieces of their lives back together—she would have to get used to doing such things on her own . . . No. She refused to think like that.

She moved on into the gold rush era that was such an important part of Canada's heritage. Descending a mineshaft, she shivered at the chill air produced by water dripping and splashing off a massive cedar water wheel. But she felt a different sort of chill at the sawmill.

She stopped to examine the jagged teeth of the open blade stopped midway into slicing a giant log. What interesting patterns—she jumped in alarm when it whirred into sudden life with a screeching cry. How could she have been standing so close to that? She turned and fled out to the harbor scene.

With everything so realistic she shouldn't have been surprised when the seagulls flapped and cried, but she had to restrain herself from throwing her arms up as protection.

She turned and stumbled aboard a 200-year-old sailing vessel, the HMS *Discovery*. Other visitors milled around the display, chatting, but she felt isolated and vulnerable. As if one of the passersby might grab her. Silly, but that buzz saw had spooked her. She put a hand to one ear, trying to silence the high-pitched scream she still heard.

She gave herself a shake and looked around. The anthropology rooms were just ahead. That was a subject that fascinated Tom. He would be here. Leaving the Victorian elegance and industrious pioneers behind her, she entered the aboriginal world of Indians and Eskimos. A forest of totem poles rose before her. A mesmerizing drum-accompanied chant filled the air, the throbbing beat leading into a cave of supernatural power filled with ceremonial masks.

The thick blackness of the chant-echoing cave engulfed her. She could see nothing. Thrumming beats and hypnotic incantations echoed from wall to wall. And then a closer sound.

She more felt than heard the breathing behind her. More ominous than the buzz saw had been. In a headlong lunge Laura rushed from the cave. Then stopped, blinking at the sudden light. And her heart leapt. Tom. Tall and straight in his camelhair jacket, his back to her, gazing up at the highest totem pole. She hurried forward, a greeting on her lips.

He turned and held out his arms. Laura started forward, then stopped in dismay. The open arms were not for her. A small blond woman emerged from behind another pole to be engulfed in the embrace.

Chapter 4

Laura's stifled cry of anguish died in relief as the couple walked toward her. In full face the man didn't bear the slightest resemblance to Tom.

What's wrong with me? I must be coming completely unglued. Laura leaned against a roughly carved totem, forcing herself to breathe slowly to regain her composure. Without thought, a fingertip found its way to her mouth. On the second nibble she caught herself and jammed her hand into her pocket. *Concentrate on your work.*

Going down the escalator Laura pulled out her pen and headed a new page: Living Land, Living Sea—natural history of British Col—. . . The title ended in a scrawl as she lost her balance on the moving stairway and her tired, aching left arm dropped her books. The whole pile scattered the length of the escalator.

She lunged for her books, forgetting the stairway was still moving. The double momentum hurled her heavily down the final steps toward an ominous crash-landing.

"Careful, ma'am." A pair of strong hands reached out to catch her midfall. "Writing on an escalator is a dangerous occupation."

"Yes. Yes, it is." Laura struggled for her composure and her balance. "Thank you. Everyone here is so friendly and helpful."

Her rescuer placed her on firm footing and began gathering her belongings. "Are you going to the exhibits? Let me carry these books for you."

"Oh, er—" Laura looked at the man's dark curly hair and the memory clicked. "We met last night, didn't we? At the airport?"

He laughed. "Lugging suitcases, hauling books—you some kind of a bodybuilding nut?"

"Hardly. Just a little disorganized, I'm afraid."

"I could carry your briefcase too." He reached toward her shoulder strap.

"Oh, no thanks—it's just part of me. I wear it like my clothes." She moved forward.

"This your first visit to the museum?"

"Yes, it's wonderful."

"It is, isn't it. I come here every chance I get. The collection started in the basement of the Parliament Building at the turn of the century. They built all this about 25 years ago. It's been rated one of the top 10 museums in the world."

"I'll bet it's even higher than that." Laura fell into step beside her book-bearer and guide.

"Some say its number two—after Mexico's."

"And just think—that's a national museum. This one's just for a province. That's really amazing. Do you live here?"

Laura's escort started to explain about his business that brought him to Victoria from Calgary and how a changed appointment had left him with the morning free for museum-browsing, but just then they rounded a corner and Laura's startled, "Oh!" brought them to a standstill. A giant woolly mammoth loomed before them, its yards-long tusks curving out menacingly toward Laura. "Oh, my goodness, that's impressive."

When she had her breath back, they walked on through the land that was now Vancouver Island recreated as it was aeons before humankind first set foot there: bird-filled, cedar-scented forest with elk and deer behind every tree; the rugged, Pacific coast with seal and walrus sporting on the rocks; tidal marshes populated with great blue heron, magnificient snow geese, and the now nearly extinct snow-white black-billed trumpeter swan. Laura's arm appreciated not having to carry her heavy package, but another part of her resented the stranger's presence beside her. If she couldn't have Tom, she didn't want anybody.

Last stop was a special room dedicated to the history of the Canadian Mountie—from horse and saddle to Harley-Davidson with sidecar. Ink flowed across Laura's page, then she capped her pen and reached for her books. "Thank you. I do feel more rested now."

He hesitated. "I'd be more than happy to carry these to your room for you."

Laura grasped the package firmly. "I'm fine, thank you. Good luck with your business meetings." She walked briskly toward the door.

Outside, she hurried across Thunderbird Court toward the Crystal Garden. That had been the next stop on her itinerary. *Would Tom remember? Would Tom care?* She looked right and left, hoping to spot him. *What a stupid thing not to be more precise about where we'd meet and when. Typical of me, but not like Tom to be vague about arrangements. Did he do it on purpose to avoid spending the morning with me? What has he been doing all morning? Who has he been talking to? Or was he somewhere in the museum? Should she go back and check?*

She turned and took a step back. Then saw that man—they hadn't even exchanged names, but she thought of him as Monty, having just come from the Royal Canadian Mounted Police exhibit. There he stood, just outside the museum, watching her. Laura whirled back around swiftly.

"In a hurry, lady?" A tall male form loomed in front of her.

"I've been waiting here for close on an hour. But I guess it was too much to hope you'd be looking for me. After all, you had plenty to occupy you in the museum."

"Oh, Tom! I was thinking about you so hard I didn't see you. Yes, the museum was great. Why didn't you come in? I told you I'd go to the period rooms—there's all these rooms you walk through—it's like really being there in history. And it's all hands-on—you can touch everything."

"Everything? Even the visitors?"

He didn't say it like a joke, but Laura laughed anyway. It was so good to be with him, even if he was in a cross mood. "Come on, let's see the gardens and have tea. You know, when in Victoria, drink tea like the Victorians." Laura led the way into the long, flag-lined brick building with the high, glass-domed roof. Tom followed silently.

They were welcomed by two vibrant red jungle birds swinging and chirping shrilly in their ornate gold cage. Laura bent close to the filigree bars. "Hello, there. You're very cheery, aren't you?" She stood and turned to Tom. "I have to remind myself the birds in here are real. Everything in the museum was stuffed and mounted, but it seemed so lifelike."

"Looked real enough to me."

"What? You mean you were *there?* And we didn't find each other? Oh, Tom, I'm so sorry."

"Are you?" He gave her his searing look that never failed to quell the most formidable opponent across a bargaining table.

Laura started to assure him of her contrition, but at that moment they stepped under the crystal roof and entered an exotic jungle paradise. "Oh, flamingos. Aren't they beautiful?" Laura grabbed Tom by the arm and practically drug him along the pebbled path to where a stand of long-legged, bright coral birds drank and fluffed their feathers at a private tropical pool. "Look—there—on one spindly leg—the Stead-fast Tin Soldier." She dashed a quick note, hardly noticing that Tom didn't reply.

They moved on through the lush vegetation: broad-leafed rain forest trees overhead and vivid flowers along the paths. "Look. Aren't those the bluest birds you've ever seen?" She pointed and pulled on Tom's arm, feeling as if she were leading a somnambulist around—and a wooden one at that. But she was determined to break through his barrier. The real Tom was still in there somewhere—if she could just reach him.

Hyacinth Macaw a plaque on a low wall read. Laura grabbed her pen to record the details of the exotic birds: indigo feathers with electric yellow on their beaks and encircling their eyes. "Isn't it wonderful! Every tiniest detail of creation done with care. Just for the pure joy of beauty."

Tom viewed the magnificent birds so stoically Laura wanted to quip that the animals were real but the visitors were stuffed and mounted. Even in his most left-brained, number-crunching mode he wasn't usually this stiff. Why was he so distant? She hurried on before her mind could form the forbidden answer: Marla.

They sat by a pool and watched Japanese carp and goldfish swim; walked past banks of bright hibiscus, fuchsia, and appropriately named flamingo flowers. They paused at a waterfall where small, green-winged tea ducks; electric orange goldfish; and one chartreuse, turquoise, and red parrot made their homes. Then they crossed the curving, vine-trailed bamboo bridge to the aviary where a whole beauty pageant of salmon-crested cockatoos preened for admirers and long-billed scarlet ibis fed.

Laura's pen moved. "Now *that's* scarlet." She tipped her head to one side. "I wonder how they ever get the food all the way up that slender bill to their throats."

No reply. She might as well have been accompanying a stone statue. She couldn't believe he didn't even respond when they rounded the corner and met Chiquita and Pedro, tiny marmoset monkeys. The little balls of fur bounced from branch to branch and scrutinized their visitors through bright round eyes. And Tom smiled. Almost.

However small, this was a victory she could follow up on. "Let's eat." She nudged him toward a bamboo gazebo overlooking the sunken garden. Fans turned languidly in the high, crystal firmament, echoing the gently waving palms around them. They sat under a flowering hibiscus tree while Concerto for Waterfall and Macaw played in the background. Laura dumped her books on the floor. "Oh, it feels so good to be rid of those books. Stupid me, I've been lugging them around all day."

"Oh? Really?"

Did he think she was needling him for not offering to take them? "Oh, that's OK. Actually I did have a little reprieve in the museum. You'll never believe—" Then she saw the coldness in his look. "Tom! You were in the museum. Why didn't you say something?"

"You looked perfectly content. I had no intention of playing odd man out with your gigolo."

"My *what?* Don't be silly, Tom. That was the merest chance meeting. You can't possibly think it was some sort of—of assignation."

Silence drowned the sound of the waterfall as the waitress set a tray of tiny sandwiches and a pot of tea in front of them. Laura poured: black for Tom, white for herself.

She shoved Tom's cup toward him, but he didn't touch it. "Or was it some sort of charade? Some infantile idea to make me jealous—which is rather what it looked like. I know you too well to think you'd seek out male companionship."

"Well, I should hope so—"

But Tom wasn't finished. "I can't even figure out why you want me around. You don't need me. You have the people in your head to talk to. I'm surprised you noticed I wasn't there."

"Of course I noticed. What do you think?"

"What difference would it have made? Would you have seen the displays any clearer with me by your side? Or is that why you latched on to Lothario—because you didn't have me to play Kendrick for you?"

"Kevin. My hero's name is Kevin. But what are you saying? Are you jealous of my fictional people?"

Tom shrugged. "Of course not. Why should I be?" The irony in his voice said the reasons were so obvious it would be ridiculous to mention them.

Did Tom feel shut out of her life? She complained because he didn't tell her about his business deals. But how much did she tell him about her stories? But he wasn't interested. Tom never read novels. He wouldn't understand.

Anyway, none of that mattered. The overwhelming fact was that Tom cared. *He cares. He cares enough to be jealous.* She was shaking so with excitement she couldn't get her teacup to her mouth. "Oh, Tom, thank you. Thank you."

"Thank you? For what? For spending one of the worst mornings of my life while my wife goes on a sight-seeing jaunt with some greasy stranger?"

"But that's just it—he *is* a stranger. I don't even know his name. It's not as if I knew him, er—intimately, like you and Marla—" Her hand flew to her mouth. She hadn't meant to say that. She hadn't even been thinking about Marla. Not actively, that is; she was always there subliminally.

But then a glimmer of a new thought pushed its way in.

45

"Oh, Tom. I see. Is that how it was with you? Something that looked bad but was totally meaningless? Oh, Tom . . ."

The rest of the day Laura moved encased in a gold-spun cloud made of her happy thoughts: *Tom cares for me. I see how it was with Marla. Tom cares. My husband cares. Oh, Tom, Tom, that's all I need to know. We can go on now.*

Tonight. We'll start tonight. This will be the first night of our honeymoon—the honeymoon we should have had seven years ago. Tom, I love you so much. I'll show you tonight—really show you. I'll be all yours . . .

Laura reveled in the luxury of having a suite. While Tom worked at the Chippendale escritoire in the living room, she splashed happily in the oversized tub, then lavished herself with the imported powder and perfume she had purchased at the hotel gift shop. The ivory satin of her gown shimmered as she slipped it over her head. She had bought it with considerable trepidation just before leaving home. She had never worn such a thing before, but she knew she simply could not allow herself to bring her favorite blue flannel pajamas on a honeymoon. Although she did slip a cotton granny gown into her suitcase in a last-minute panic.

She hummed softly to herself as she brushed her hair to a glow that matched her gown and her eyes. The golden cloud moved with her as she glided into the living room and stood behind Tom, smiling gently.

She raised her arm to reach out and caress the back of his neck. But her arm froze midmotion. Panic tightened her throat, her breath came short, her hands sweaty. Suddenly there was a third person in the room.

"Laura, put your robe on!" her mother ordered through tight lips. Laura reached woodenly for the terry cloth robe she had tossed across the love seat earlier. *"And fasten it."* Laura tied the belt. Then, because there were no buttons, she held

the lapels together at her throat. The specter surveyed her severely, then melted with the last wisps of Laura's golden cloud.

"I—I'll see you in bed, Tom." Her voice was as tight as her mother's had been. She hoped it wasn't as disapproving. She fled around the corner and up the steps to the bedroom.

Her fingers so tense her pen would hardly move, Laura poured her soul-searching into her journal: *What's wrong with me? I don't understand. I tried so hard. I was so determined tonight would be different. And I prayed. Over and over again— "Please, God, don't let it be a disaster." Is this His answer?*

No, I can't blame this on anyone else—not on Marla, not on Tom, not on God. It's all my fault. I'm to blame. I can't make love to my husband, and it's all my fault. I must be guilty of some terrible character flaw. Or maybe I'm insane. I know my reactions aren't normal, and it seems the harder I try to fight them, the worse I get . . .

"I'm going downstairs to get a newspaper." At the sound of Tom's voice Laura jumped and clutched her robe to her. The look of disgust that crossed his face at her reflex brought stinging tears to Laura's eyes, but she was beyond being able to cope with her emotions.

She lay in stiff silence in the big bed and wondered how long it could possibly take to buy a newspaper in the lobby . . . how long . . . how . . . She finally fell asleep beneath the elegant Georgian canopy, her new ivory satin gown buried under layers of covers.

Chapter 5

Laura wakened to the sound of seagulls outside the window, a small reminder that they were on an island. And then she looked at the small island that was their bed. There was Tom, boyish and vulnerable in his sleep. Her first impulse was to nudge him awake and ask, "Where were you last night?" But the joy of waking to his presence beside her erased much of the desperate emptiness of the night before. Besides, she wasn't sure she wanted to know the answer.

She *was* sure though, that she didn't want to rouse any conflict. It was so awful—this fear of talking freely to Tom. All because of the specter he had raised between them.

And the specter she raised between them. She had to admit it. Could she ever break down those barriers or find a way around them? Somehow she must. She must find her way to Tom. Back to Tom as it had been in the beginning. She closed her eyes and savored their early days together: laughing, touching, kissing; getting to know each other, love each other, trust each other . . .

Our first kiss, strolling through the park at twilight in early spring. The sky was pink, the air heavy-sweet from flowering locust trees, and we were the only people in the world. Certainly the only two who had ever been so much in love. Metallic clangs and children's laughter from the playground rang a carillon in the background. We stopped by a screen of tall junipers, his arm tightened on my shoulder. He bent his head to me. It was the most completely right moment in my life.

She lay there, reliving the moment again and again. In that supreme moment, Tom had gone beyond words to find a way to say, *I care.* It was a celebration of their attraction for each other, of their love, of their future together. From that time his kisses became events of complete communication, of sensitivity, of sharing something from deep within themselves. It was a few months after the wedding that it dawned on her; in marriage hugging and kissing always led to something else.

Without realizing it, her breathing constricted and she pulled the sheet tight under her chin.

Even with all the problems and all the failures, though, they had managed to build something together that had lasted seven years. Hardly a lifetime, but it was something—a good start. And in spite of everything, they had been seven good years—lots of sharing and companionship, lots of laughter, lots of success in their careers and community service. Too much to give up, to consign to the ash heap, to allow to become just another statistic of separation—or worse. She wouldn't even allow herself to think the *D* word.

She slid out of bed, buoyed with a fresh determination for the new day. Clicking on the TV as she passed it, she went on into the bathroom. She had just finished brushing her teeth when Tom called to her. "Want to eat in the Garden Court again this morning, or shall I ring for room service?"

"How about tea and toast here, then a real breakfast at the gardens?" Laura finished rinsing, then started to say something more through the half-open door.

"Sh-sh-sh." Tom shushed her and turned his attention to the local news report. Laura came into the room as it ended. "Can you imagine that? An old man mugged yesterday right in downtown Victoria. In broad daylight, no less."

Laura shuddered. "It doesn't seem possible in such a beautiful place, but I guess no place is safe these days."

"Or any days. There was a serpent in the Garden of Eden, remember."

"And that's where we're going today—the ultimate garden!" She flung out her arms.

Tom's grin let her know he was making a fresh effort today too. "Great. But watch out for serpents."

Tom was holding the door for her when the phone rang. She picked it up. "Hello . . . hello?" She shrugged at the silent line and replaced the receiver.

They were soon heading back up Route 17, the way they had traveled to town from the airport. Laura smiled, thinking that only someone who had recently been airsick could appreciate how good it felt to have both feet on the ground—or at least all four tires. Then she glanced over at the instrument panel. "Eighty! You're not driving *eighty?*"

"Kilometers."

"Oh, a metric speedometer. Cute."

"Well, you wanted a foreign setting, didn't you?"

"Exotic at least. Canada isn't really foreign—except their system of weights and measures."

"But then, admit it—you never coped too well with miles and pounds."

Laura giggled. "Too right-brained, I know."

"Yeah, you hear of people with two left feet. Sometimes I think you've got two right brains."

"Of course. That's why I'm so intuitive and creative and such an all-around wonderful person."

"And such a math whiz."

"Well, you can't have everything."

Tom's gentle smile transformed the sharpness of his features. "So will you please explain to my left-brained self why the big deal about flowers in your book?"

"Not flowers—roses."

"I thought roses were flowers."

"Shakespeare was a playwright. Not all playwrights are Shakespeare."

"A metaphor even I can understand."

She thought for a moment. "You know, that's about the only way you can express it. Who really knows why roses are so special? Why for centuries has the rose so inspired poets, lovers, and artists? Somehow it's always been the symbol of the superlative, of pure character, of rich meaning.

"The Victorians had a whole code of rose language: a red rose said I love you; a white rose said I am worthy of you; a yellow rose was for declining love; red and white roses together were for unity." She paused. "I guess it's like love itself—only the heart can define the beauty of a rose."

Ever since Laura could remember she had had an indefinable desire to surround herself with beauty, especially with roses. She had never questioned it. Who wouldn't want such exquisite loveliness around them? But now she wondered if it could have anything to do with her hurt over not being beautiful herself—as if she might somehow then bear a reflection of the beauty around her. She glanced in the visor mirror and sighed. If that was her goal, it hadn't worked.

They left the main highway and followed the sign of a single red rose to a green, wooded country lane winding gently through rolling grasses and thickets. As soon as they entered that bowered world, Laura knew she would find something very special at the end of the road.

And, indeed, she did. Bordered walks, blossomed mounds, and overflowing baskets flowered everywhere. And they hadn't even come to the gardens yet. Already Laura felt overwhelmed—how was she ever going to describe this in her book: the freshness of the air, the unique floral scent, the riotous banks of color? She couldn't begin to take it all in herself. How could she possibly translate it? With a sense of helplessness she followed Tom to the Greenhouse Restaurant.

They sat on wrought iron chairs under hanging baskets heavy with blooms, surrounded by flower-entwined trellised walls. Tom brought their breakfast from the buffet: a thick slab of baked country ham with homemade bread, freshly squeezed orange juice, and richly brewed breakfast tea.

Laura nibbled a piece of dry toast. "I can't cope with this—this sensory overload. How can I ever grasp it?"

"Try reducing it to lists."

"That sounds terribly cold and inartistic, but I'll try." Her pen moved: begonias, fuchsias . . . She hesitated at the baskets filling the trellis arches. It was like meeting a long-lost acquaintance and feeling one should recognize them.

Suddenly it clicked. "Tom, do you realize those are impatiens?"

"I know the feeling."

"No, silly, the flowers. But look at their size. Each blossom must be six times as big as they grow at home."

Tom nodded and glanced at his watch. "That's great. But what time do you meet this Glen fellow?" Laura had made an appointment to interview a horticulturist.

"One o'clock in the rose garden. That gives us plenty of time to do some of the other gardens first."

Tom glanced at the map. "Right. What'll it be?"

"The sunken garden is the one most often featured in pictures. But I'm not sure it matters. A riot is a riot—"

"—is a riot." Tom finished. "Since a rose is a rose is a rose has already been said."

"Yes, but Gertrude Stein didn't see Butchart Gardens or she'd have known the flowers here are unlike any others in the world."

Tom helped her with her chair and handed her her briefcase. "Good grief, woman, what do you have in here?"

She shrugged. "Just the necessities. Books, maps, paper . . ." Funny, he wouldn't have thought the weight unnecessary if the papers had borne statistics instead of poetic descriptions.

They followed the path past a multigabled birdhouse, between hillsides of shamrocks, and beneath tall pines to the former rock quarry—its walls a solid English ivy green, its floor a maze of colored mounds of yellow and orchid chrysanthemums, red and pink, orange and blue . . .

Standing at the top of the quarry wall, Laura's mind boggled. Well, if she couldn't cope visually, she'd try approaching it aurally. She closed her eyes and heard the tumbling of a slender waterfall at the far end of the garden, a gentle click, click of cameras, the hushed whispers of people as overcome as herself, behaving as if they were entering a great cathedral.

She took Tom's arm and they entered the enchanted world together, the sun warm on their heads like a benediction. *Let it be that,* Laura thought. *A blessing on our love.* As her amen she squeezed Tom's arm.

His sudden jerking away was like a slap in the face. She recoiled to the other side of the walkway. Why were they never on an even footing? Just when she thought they'd found common ground it all fell away under her feet. Well, if that was how he wanted it, she needed to focus on the flowers anyway. She stopped beside a bed of begonias—tuberous and fibrous both—species that had defied all her horticultural attempts at home. But at least she could revel in their beauty here—a small hillside of vibrant yellow, coral, and pink.

"This cool, moist climate gives such intensity to the colors." Yesterday when she had voiced her thoughts Tom hadn't been there to hear them. This had to be progress, she assured herself, even if his hand at her elbow urging her on ahead of an approaching tour group was cold and impersonal.

The next bed was silvery dusty miller growing against spiky red salvia and fuzzy blue ageratum. "One of Jenny Butchart's greatest gifts was her artist's eye for the most spectacular color arrangements. I read that she won a scholarship to study art in Paris but chose to marry Mr. Butchart instead." Laura paused.

"Isn't life funny? She probably thought she was giving up her art when she made that decision, but I don't suppose she could ever have achieved so much or left such a legacy of art to the world if she had pursued her career. I think Gwendolyn needs to see that." She jotted a note. "You know, Kevin—" She choked as she saw the strange way her husband was regarding her. Had she done it again? Shut him out for her story line? But he was the one who had drawn away from her at the top of the path.

In the midst of all the light and beauty around her, Laura felt overcome with darkness and ugliness. Fears and remembered failings rose higher than the stone cliffs surrounding the garden. Why wasn't loving and caring enough? Why wasn't praying to do better enough? She wanted the rock quarry of their marriage to bloom like this garden, but how did one go about it?

"Tom—?"

"Well, at least you got my name right this time." He strode on to the edge of the lagoon. Its still, black waters reflected craggy rocks, graceful willows, and the touches of red and gold foliage that the cool nights were adding to the color scheme.

Only that morning Laura had recalled a long-ago moment she and Tom spent in another park. In her mind she reached out to him, took his hand, and they strolled on through this garden in the perfect harmony they had known before the demands of marriage intruded. As if sensing her desire, Tom moved just beyond her reach, his hands clenched tightly together behind him.

Laura sighed and turned her back on the lagoon. The path wandered through more beds of begonias while above them autumn trees bordered the garden, all mingling their reds, yellows, and oranges, mixing and blending like the softly spoken languages of the many nations she heard around her.

"You know, I was afraid October would be too late in the year, but it's even more beautiful with colored foliage." If Tom turned from her touch, at least she could reach out with words.

"Yes. Very colorful. I had no idea it would be like this." His reply was stiff, but Laura could have turned handsprings. He did like it. In his subdued way, Tom was appreciating the beauty around him. If only they could be experiencing it together—*really* together. If only they could experience marriage *really* together. Just walking through Butchart Gardens distanced from Tom but imagining what it would be like if they were really together like the characters in her head was a painful but important lesson. The trouble was, she knew how her story would end. Life was so uncertain. Still, there was nothing to do but keep going.

The path curved around another flowerbed, then offered them a bench fronted by banks of marigolds where they could sit and watch the fountain play in the lagoon before the limestone mountain wall. "Research size of fountain," Laura wrote in the margin of her notes.

"This is the 70-foot Ross fountain installed in 1964 and named in honor of Ian Ross, Mrs. Butchart's grandson who ran the gardens." Laura gasped in astonishment as the tour guide behind her unwittingly supplied her needed information as he lectured his group. "Ross received these gardens for his 21st birthday after the provincial government refused to buy them for one dollar."

Laura nudged Tom. "Talk about a real estate investment opportunity." He acknowledged her comment with raised eyebrows.

Along the upper level of the quarry garden they walked past rows of maple trees. Laura raised her face to the autumn leaves glowing a hot orangy-red in the sun. "Now we know we're really in Canada. I'll bet maple leaves don't turn that color anywhere else in the world."

Tom nodded. "Exactly the color on the Canadian flag. You have to see it to believe it's real."

In appreciation at Tom's response, Laura reached out to him—just long enough for her to feel the warmth of his body and the rough texture of his tweed jacket on her cheek. Then he pulled away. Laura stared at his back. *It's almost as if he's afraid to touch me or to be alone with me. As if he were the one who dreaded—um, er—intimacy.* Even in her thoughts she wasn't going to use the three-letter word for marital passion. Her mother once had all but scrubbed the skin off her tongue washing her mouth out with soap. Once was enough.

And yet that painful, hurt look remained in Tom's eyes. That was entirely ridiculous, because Tom was the one who had hurt her.

Right. Back to the scene at hand. Purple-leafed Persian plum trees behind a wall of hydrangeas and a festivity of Canterbury bells. "You can almost hear them ring, can't you?"

No response. As if he were punishing her. But for what?

They crossed the broad green concert lawn where musicals were staged in the summer and fireworks displays held in July and August. "Oh, Tom, wouldn't that be fun? We must come back!" If there was still a "we" by next summer.

Tom ignored the implications of her statement. "Just time for lunch before your appointment. Shall we skip the Japanese garden?"

"It's only over that little hill. Can we walk through it really fast?"

Tom strode out, not bothering to reply. The austerely formal, clipped atmosphere of Oriental restraint was like a cool shower after the baroque riot of the sunken garden. Everything was held in perfect, unemotional order, the only color provided by the fall foliage and a curved red footbridge. Nothing bloomed. *I know how it feels.* Laura nodded as she looked at the closely trimmed bonsai tree confined in the center of a dry, pebble bed neatly raked into a pattern of rippling water.

But as they climbed the stairs toward the Torri exit, a little brook beside them babbled unrestrainedly between its mossy banks. It was a thin stream singing of joy and hope, breaking from the bonds of constriction.

"Oh!" Laura's startled exclamation snapped the fragile atmosphere.

"What is it?"

She looked around, puzzled. "I don't know. Nothing, I guess. I had the impression someone was there—ready to jump at me from that bush." She shook her head. "Silly, I know."

Tom shrugged. "Writer's imagination."

They passed a star-shaped pond with stone frogs spurting into the water, then past a splashing fountain of cavorting dolphins and turned in at the sign of the little green teapot. Inside the dining room they were welcomed by a high, blazing fireplace. Laura held her hands out to the fire. "I didn't have any idea I was so cold. The sun is so bright on the flowers that it doesn't seem possible there could be such a chill in the air."

Tom asked for the warmest seat in the room, and they were led to one by a black iron stove where nearby water trickled from an Italian lavabo and, as always, flowers bloomed in profusion. Laura looked at their hostess—beautiful, gracious, and pregnant. And she was stabbed by the thought that so often crossed her mind when she saw women in that happy condition, *Does God love her more than He does me?* And as always, the thought was followed by deep contrition. She didn't mean to be blaming God for her problems. It was just that her hurt ran so deep. Laura was glad to see Tom lost in concentration over his menu; she could hope he hadn't even noticed the hostess.

Laura ordered Scotch broth and salad, then cupped her hands around her little brown teapot. "Ah, the circulation is coming back."

Tom reached across the table and touched her hand. "You are cold. Why didn't you say something?"

"Well, I didn't really realize it until I got in here. Had my mind on other things, I guess." It felt so good to have Tom holding her hand. It was what she'd been dreaming of all morning. She looked up at him with her heart in her eyes.

That was her mistake.

He pulled back as if from the metaphorical snake he had mentioned earlier. "You needn't make your calf eyes at me. Save them for Lothario. He's probably lurking somewhere behind the potted palm."

"What are you talking about?"

"Your helpful friend. I don't suppose you knew I saw him. Or are you going to tell me he's the horticulturist you're meeting this afternoon?"

"Tom. I have no idea what you're talking about."

"And I suppose you have no idea your friend from the

museum is here, even though he stood in full view waving at you."

"When? I didn't see him."

"Didn't you really? He was directly below you when we were at the top of the sunken garden."

She thought back, frowning, then gave a sputter of a laugh. "Oh! That must have been when I had my eyes closed."

"Huh?"

"I was concentrating on the sounds. I always try to work with all my senses. What is the matter with you—?"

Before she could finish her question, she knew. She had taken a course in psychology in order to better understand the workings of her characters' minds. She knew all about projection—casting one's own guilt and motives onto another, suspecting others of what one was up to oneself. Tom felt guilty about Marla, he suspected Laura of setting up a rendezvous, as he would have liked to. She bit her lip and clenched her hands together. She would not make a scene in the restaurant. This was not the place to accuse Tom of further infidelities—even if he did seem to be accusing her. "That man—whoever he is—is simply here on a business trip from Calgary."

"Has a lot of time to hit the tourist spots on his business trip, doesn't he? And if he's from Calgary, why was he on our plane from Seattle?"

"Was he? I was too busy looking for an airsick bag to notice anything."

"Yes, he was right behind you. And never more than 12 inches from you the whole time in the airport until I dealt with the matter."

"Well, thank you, Sir Galahad." She looked at the bowl of rich lamb and barley soup before her. Her stomach lurched.

"I have an appointment now. A *business* appointment, but you are more than welcome to come since I'm so untrustworthy." She pushed her chair back with a sharp scrape.

"Don't worry. I brought plenty of my own work. We'll meet at the car when you're through. You needn't rush. I have everything I need."

His dismissal rang in her ears and suppressed tears blurred her vision. Indeed, he had everything. He had a cell phone, a laptop computer with modem fax, an electronic pocket organizer, a wife, and a paramour. Who could want more?

Chapter 6

Laura forced herself to slow her steps and to breathe slower. She did not want to arrive at her interview in a flurry. She paused under the trellised archway, blossom-heavy with clusters of pink rambling roses, and took a deep breath of spicy, sweet air. Assured that she exhibited outward calm and professionalism, she entered the rose garden.

A young woman in a tan coverall was bent over pruning roses in a bed halfway along the path. "Excuse me," Laura approached her. "Can you tell me where I could find Glen Hampden?"

The young woman straightened up, pulled off her glove, and extended her hand. "I'm Glenda Hampden. You must be the writer who wants an interview?"

"Yes, I'm Laura James." All business now, Laura put her personal turmoil aside as firmly as she drew her notebook from her briefcase.

"Good. Let's sit over here by the gazing ball."

Laura couldn't believe her fortune! She had made the appointment to learn background for her rose-grower heroine—and here was a real-life horticulturist made to order: soft brown pageboy with auburn lights, sprinkling of freckles across a pert little nose, a smile that made you think you heard children laughing. Laura's pen moved even as she sat on a cement bench beside a pedestaled crystal ball reflecting a web of sunshine around them.

"You'll have to forgive my surprise; I was expecting a man.

Narrow-minded of me, I suppose. Anyway, I'm glad you're not."

Glenda smiled and nodded. "There are several women on the staff. Most women horticulturists seem to prefer working in greenhouses, but I want to be here with my roses."

"Yes, that's what I would choose too. They are gorgeous. What are your favorites?"

"I love them all, but of course, you do develop favorites. Roses are living things; they have personalities just like pets or even people. I like roses I can go into the garden and smell—like Double Delight and the David Austin English roses. Of course, I get my share of scratches, but it's worth it."

"You're getting the garden ready for winter?" It sounded like chitchat, but Laura would need to know these things about her Gwendolyn's work.

"We will soon. The pruning I'm doing now is really just cosmetic—for the tourists. If this was my own garden, I wouldn't be pruning this time of year."

"You don't prune for winter?"

"We do here, because it looks better. But I would let the old blooms form hips and seal the canes. When you prune for winter you leave an open wound and frost can just go right down the cane. Besides, you can use the rose hips for tea or jelly in the spring—great source of vitamin C, you know."

"Will you mulch for winter?"

"Yes, that's my next job. We mound mushroom manure well up over the graft."

"Mushroom manure? I've never heard of it."

"We get it from mushroom growers. It's the richest mulch we can find. We don't use straw because it draws the phosphate from the soil, and then it all has to be hauled off in the spring. The mushroom manure we can just dig in around the plants."

Laura glanced at the list of questions she had prepared ahead of time, but she found it hard to stick to business. She felt so drawn to this girl. She wanted to get to know her personally. "Where do you get your roses?"

"Everywhere, really. Some of the big growers in America are great, but really, we need a Canadian rose grower. Getting the rootstock across the border is an awful hassle. If the inspector finds any bugs, he'll torch the whole lot. You can easily lose $10,000 at a whack that way."

"Is it any easier to get roses from England?"

"It's really a matter of where the rose you want is. If it's in Timbuktu, you go for it. And keep your fingers crossed for the ag customs officers."

Laura looked at her next question. "What do you feed them?"

Glenda stood up. "Albert, he's our head gardener, said I could talk all I wanted, but I should work while I do it. You don't mind, do you?"

"Not at all." Laura stood too. "I'll just follow you around. I want to get a real feel for what you do."

Glenda pulled on her gloves and extended her hands. "Sheepskin. They're special to protect from the thorns." She picked up a pair of orange-handled shears. "Good sharp clippers are important. These are English. The best." She scooted a hard plastic bucket along the path, making a harsh, scraping sound. "There, Albert will hear that and know I'm making progress with my clipping." She tossed a faded rose in the bucket.

"You asked about feeding. We mix our own 6-8-6 formula with plenty of trace elements and Epsom salts. Then feed one tablespoon per plant."

"Epsom salts?"

Glenda nodded. "Because we get so much rain here. It

cleanses the soil, prevents root rot. Good drainage is absolutely essential."

Laura was writing as fast as her pen would move. She couldn't wait to get home and try all this on her own bushes. Except the Epsom salts—hardly necessary in the desert land around Boise.

"Of course, we spray religiously—insecticide, fungicide—and don't water from overhead. That awful rain the other night just demolished these blooms. You're not seeing our garden at its best at all. But then, if the rain doesn't get them the deer will. See—hoofprints in the soil right here."

Laura was amazed. "This close to people?"

"Oh, yes. They come in at night. Here's more prints. And in the spring it's rabbits. They're worse because they eat the new shoots."

The bucket scraped on the path, Glenda's clippers snapped, other tourists strolled through the garden admiring the roses and asking Glenda brief questions about rose growing. A visitor picked up a rosebud from the bucket. "May I take one?"

"Oh, I'm sorry. Those are for my compost pile. If I gave them all away, I wouldn't have anything to feed the pile." The lady dropped the rose and moved on. Glenda smiled at Laura. "I probably say that 10 times a day. It would be nice to give them away, but we use everything here."

Laura walked on a ways by herself, then turned back. "This is the only rose garden I've ever seen that gives the date and nation of the rose's origin as well as its name."

"Yeah, that's interesting, isn't it? The signs are about 98 percent correct. Some young interns did them. They made a few mistakes. Someday maybe we'll have time to redo them."

"Are there many from Canada?"

"Just one. Jenny Butchart is the only Canadian rose developed."

"Was it done here?"

"No. We don't have room to hybridize. Wish we did, though."

Laura walked along, reading the markers: Cathedral, Ireland, 1975; Sir Lancelot, England, 1967; Fragrant Cloud, Germany; Anne Cocker, Scotland; Holland, Denmark, Belgium, Japan . . . It was a United Nations of roses. "Mountbatten. That's not marked, but it has to be English." She turned back toward Glenda.

"Yes, it is. It's a really good yellow rose—deep color. Yellow roses are favorites of mine, but they need more sun. The ones on that side of the garden get too much shade. They'll have to be moved."

"Oh, here's Peace. One of my favorites. I didn't know it was developed in France."

"Yes, it has quite a history. It was developed just before the Nazi invasion. Francis Meilland smuggled three packages to other countries. Two were confiscated by the Nazis, but one reached the States. It was officially named Peace on April 29, 1945—the day Berlin fell. It was given the American Rose Society's award the day the war with Japan ended. And when the peace treaty was signed, it was given a gold medal."

For a moment Laura was too engrossed to write, even though she would need this information later. "I had no idea. I just thought it got its name from its soothing blend of colors."

"Ouch." Glenda's cry interrupted Laura's peaceful musings. "Not much gets through these gloves, but that one's a beaut. They're a lot worse this year—cold winters make the bushes produce more thorns. Last year was about the worst we've ever had—some bushes just went all to thorns."

Glenda looked at her watch. "Teatime. Care for a cuppa?"

"I'd love it." The time in the rose garden had been so calming. Laura didn't want to recall that she had been too upset to eat her lunch.

They went to a long glass greenhouse just beyond the public gardens, but thoroughly secluded from public view by a screen of trees and bushes. "I had no idea this was here."

"That's the idea. We have eight or nine greenhouses, and they're all well hidden. I think visitors are supposed to believe the fairies grow the flowers." Glenda laughed and tossed her gold-streaked auburn hair.

Laura was delighted with the information she'd received—both for her book and for use in her own garden—but she couldn't shake the feeling that what she really wanted was to get better acquainted with Glenda herself. She sought for a way to bring the conversation from roses to the rose grower. "Where did you go to school?"

"I got my horticultural degree at Windsor—King's College. I'd like to go to Guelph for some advanced work. It's the top school, but it's in Ontario, and I hate to go so far away now—" She sighed and took a sip of her cuppa. "I just don't know." She finished with an indeterminate shrug of her shoulders.

"Um," Laura searched for another question that might give the girl a chance to open up to her. "When do you get your vacation?"

"My holiday? Anytime but planting time. Growing season isn't a good time to be gone either. Now to April is good. I have two days off coming to me. I keep hoping the bugs will take some days off, too, but it never works out that way." Glenda hesitated. "I was hoping I'd need a few days of vacation—for something really important. But it doesn't look likely." She took a sip from her steaming teacup. "Mmm. Hot in here, isn't it?" She unzipped her coverall and pushed the collar back.

The gesture revealed a small gold fish hanging from a slim chain around her neck. "Oh, me too." Laura held out her hand to show her ring with a similar engraving on the band.

The women smiled at each other in recognition like first-century believers who used the symbol as a secret code. "I wonder . . ." Glenda hesitated. "Maybe you're just the person I've been looking for. I need someone to talk to. And all our friends here are really more Kyle's friends than mine, so I don't feel comfortable going to them . . ."

Nearly an hour later Laura hurried toward the car, her mind whirling with the remarkable conversation she and Glenda had just had. "Tom, thank you for waiting so patiently. You can't imagine what's happened." She jumped in beside him.

He looked up from his screen and blinked as if trying to figure out who she was. He methodically saved his work, turned off the computer, and lowered the screen. "Well, you look excited."

"I am. It's absolutely incredible—one of those truth is stranger than fiction things that I couldn't use in a novel plot because nobody would believe it. But the Glen I thought I was meeting turned out to be Glenda, and she's absolutely Gwendolyn—looks like her, knows everything about roses, *and* she's having romance problems!"

"Which you, in the best fairy godmother tradition, can solve for her." Tom started the car.

"Well, no. As a matter of fact, it may be rather the reverse." She wasn't ready to travel that conversational path yet, so she hurried on. "I can guarantee to solve Gwen's, but not Glenda's. But it did help for her to have someone to talk to."

Tom turned onto the highway toward Victoria. "So, are you going to let me in on the agitations of Glenda/Gwendolyn?"

"Not if you're going to be snide about it." It was his tone, really. And she so needed this conversation to go well. So much depended on the right lead-up.

"Sorry."

"Right. That's better. Glenda met Kyle at church when she first came here more than a year ago. It was love at first sight—at least on her part. They've been dating ever since, and Glenda's feelings have been growing all this time."

"Blossoming like her roses."

Laura bit her lip.

"OK, sorry. Didn't mean to scoff."

Laura continued, but in a subdued tone. She had to be so careful what she said. And how she said it. "She's sure Kyle loves her, but she can't get him to make a commitment. You see, he's a psychiatrist—specializing in marriage counseling—" She rushed on, not daring to look at Tom, as much as she wanted to know how he would react to that information. "Whenever they talk about their own relationship, he says he sees so many messed-up marriages he's not going to get married until he can give the relationship all the attention it really needs."

"Hmm."

"The thing is, his parents died a couple of years ago, and he has the sole responsibility for raising his kid brother—15 years old and terribly mixed up. Glenda says he's enormously bright—which may be a lot of his problem. He's bored in school, in with a bad group of friends. Kyle suspects some of them may be into drugs . . ."

"Glenda must be in love if she's willing to take on a mess like that."

"Of course she is. That's one of her main points for wanting to get married now, so she could really help Kyle—share his problems. She wouldn't try to be a mother to Darren, more of a big sister, but she's sure she could help. As it is, Darren seems to think she's interfering when she's around, since there's nothing official between her and Kyle."

"Sounds like a plot complication made to order. What's Gwendolyn going to do?"

"Oh, Gwendolyn will probably do something absolutely heroic, like leading the investigation against the drug pushers and rescuing the kid just before he shoots a fatal dose of heroin, whereupon both he and Kevin will swear they can't live without her another moment. If only things were that simple for Glenda."

"It doesn't sound very simple."

"No, waiting for life to straighten itself out and praying for guidance *sound* much simpler—but they're probably the hardest things in the world." Laura moved closer to her husband, admiring, as always, his crisp, clean look, his clear profile.

And telling you all that was the easy part for me. Now I've got to get this around to us. How can I do it without erecting a wall or igniting an explosion? Give me the words—just some way to start.

"What did you mean when you said the fairy godmother role may be reversed?"

Laura gasped. Why did answers always seem such a shock? She'd asked, hadn't she? She took a deep breath. She had her opening; there was no going back now. "Well, I meant Glenda might be able to help me. Tom, I want so desperately to make you happy. And I know I don't." Her hand touched his arm. He didn't shrug it away. "Like I said, Kyle is a marriage counselor. This whole thing could be made in heaven. Literally. You don't mind if I make an appointment to see him, do you?"

They were at a stop sign, so Tom could take his eyes from the road and really look at Laura. There was no anger, only confusion. "What are you saying, Laura? You don't really think you need professional help, do you?"

"I don't know anything else to do." Her voice broke. "I want to make you happy."

Laura hummed softly as she brushed her hair. Tonight would be different. Last night had been the dark before the dawning. In the glow of Tom's new mellowness on the drive back and the confidence of having an appointment with Dr. Kyle Larsen for the next morning, Laura was determined to strew their bed with metaphorical rosebuds, to blossom full-blown under her husband's caresses . . .

Her mind whirled with images from the garden. Tom had been so prickly that morning, but as Glenda pointed out, a cold winter produced thorns. And Tom had held on through seven cold winters. Now some of the expert advice she received on rose nurturing she would apply to husband nurturing as well. She sprayed a mist of floral-scented perfume on her hair and went into the sitting room.

Tom was at the small desk, talking on the phone and jotting figures on a pad of paper, then making squiggly doodles down the sheet. ". . . Yes, I see what you mean . . . Yes, I understand perfectly . . . Oh, yes, an enormous sum of money." He jotted more figures. "Yes, I won't forget. Good night, Marla."

Laura stood frozen to the spot, the pale green carpet hardening around her bare feet like cement. "Marla! That was Marla? *Marla?* What's she doing here?"

"Don't be ridiculous. She's not here. She called me from her office in Boise."

"I don't care where she called from. She's here. If you're

still doing business with her, she's here—right here between us!" Laura's voice rose on a hysterical note.

"Laura, be sensible." Tom stood and gripped her shoulders.

Laura tore away. "No wonder you didn't come to bed till all hours last night. No wonder you kept pulling away from me all morning. Were you on the phone to her all the time I was at my interview? You don't want me. You want her. Marla. Marla. Always Marla!"

Now Tom's anger flared to match Laura's, but he didn't shout and cry as she did. Instead, his eyes narrowed fiercely, and his voice bit with icy control. "Use your brain, woman. Think. What greater way could I possibly show my love for you than by self-denial!"

"Denial?"

"Denial. Saying no to what every electron in me was screaming for. When I was aching for you so bad I could taste it. But I knew how distasteful my lovemaking was to you. So I denied myself."

Laura shook her head against his words. "No, that's not true. I never refused. Not once. I always let you . . ."

"Let me? *Let* me! Don't you have any idea how much more there is than that? I don't want you to *let me*. I want you to *want me*. I want you to make love to me."

Laura pulled back in horror, her eyes wide with anger and fear. "I've never heard of such a thing!" Her outrage made her stutter. "A lady does not make ad-ad-advances. You—you—you want me to behave like a—a prostitute! *Is* that what you want?"

"No, Laura. I simply want to be wanted by my wife."

Clutching her robe high against her throat, Laura turned and rushed into the bathroom, locking the door behind her.

It seemed like hours later when Laura, calm but red-eyed, crept to bed. The roses she had mentally wound around the posters had wilted and the petals fallen off. Only the thorns remained.

Chapter 7

"I always feel like God is watching to see if I have my clothes on." Laura sat very straight with both feet flat on the floor, her hands clasped in her lap. Tiny beads of perspiration on her forehead betrayed the enormous effort it required for her to verbalize her feelings to Dr. Larsen sitting across from her, relaxed in a high-backed brown leather chair.

"The first thing my mother ever taught me was 'get your pants on.' She didn't put it in such crude words. It was just her long-faced attitude. 'Cover up, cover up.' I had the worst posture in the whole school. I always wore a cardigan sweater and stooped so I could pull it tighter around me." Instinctively Laura clutched at the lapels of her navy blue blazer, then forced herself to let go. Her college roommate had ridiculed her out of her slumping reflex, and she had no intention of going back to it. With a jerk she pulled her hand away from her mouth. Biting her fingernails remained to be conquered.

Kyle Larsen regarded her calmly and quietly. When it was clear she had said all she wanted to for the moment, he leaned forward and held her attention with his deep-set dark eyes behind steel-rimmed glasses. "Laura, the first thing I want you to understand is that the devil didn't invent sex. God did." He paused to allow Laura's mind to repeat the words back to herself.

She shifted in her seat, as if trying to make room for the new thought. The idea offered comfort and relaxation. And terror. Accusing God of such a thing was akin to blasphemy.

"But wouldn't any *good* girl feel like I did—do? I know the whole concept of being good is laughably old-fashioned today. Even the idea that such a thing as goodness exists is considered anti-intellectual. But postmodern thought doesn't change the truth. The farther society goes over the deep end in immorality, the more important it is that someone hold up a standard of purity."

Kyle smiled. "Let's go back to your first question. Combating deconstructionism might be a bit much to tackle in your first session. And certainly, a normal amount of modesty is a lovely virtue. But it can be out of place in the bedroom with your husband."

Laura had the lapels of her jacket clutched tight around her throat before she caught herself. She forced herself to sit back in her chair.

Kyle nodded his approval of her restored posture. "I would like to help you develop a practical theology of sexuality. You're absolutely right about society. Until a few years ago—the '60s, I suppose—sexuality was viewed in many quarters with fear and dread, as a peripheral and dangerous aspect of our lives . . ."

"Er—so who's right?"

"Like most things, truth seems to hide out somewhere in the middle. Finding the right middle is the trick. I'd like to help you find and understand the Creator's intentions for sexuality."

"Is there any doubt about that? S-s—it's for having children."

"Yes, that. But for pleasure too."

"Pleasure!" Laura was on her feet, looking around for her briefcase. She wasn't going to stay here and listen to this nonsense.

Kyle held out his hands. "Please, just hear me out." He

gestured toward the chair. "Don't think of this as counseling. Think of it as the history of philosophy."

Research. Laura could deal with that. She took her seat and pulled out her notebook. She always took notes on lectures: Greco-Roman dualism—universe divided into opposing forces: spiritual and material. Human dualism reflected both: soul—the higher spiritual nature; body—the lower, material nature. Body must battle temptations and weaknesses of the flesh so the soul could escape corruption.

"Do you see?" This could have been Professor Larsen standing in front of a university classroom. "This idea that flesh and spirit are separate and hostile is pagan, not biblical. Unfortunately it was promoted by the sainted Augustine who taught that the greatest threat to spirituality—to developing the higher nature—was sexual intercourse. It was Augustine's idea that intercourse should be engaged in only for procreation and then only in a manner that did not bring pleasure. The idea that it is a sin to enjoy the marriage bed comes from Augustine and the pagan world. Don't blame it on God."

The notebook snapped shut. "Are you trying to tell me I have a spiritual problem?" If anyone had a spiritual problem, it was this so-called doctor. Imagine saying such things about God. She was amazed the man wasn't struck by lightning before her very eyes.

"The fact of the matter is that marriages die spiritually first, but this was just a history lesson, remember?"

. . . Was Tom right? Did Monty really find me attractive? Of course not, he was just being polite to a visitor, like all Canadians . . .

"Mrs. James?"

She jumped. "Sorry. Terrible habit. What did you say?"

"I asked if you like to read poetry."

"I love it."

"Good. I want you to read the Song of Solomon."

"I've read it."

"And your voice sounds like you disapprove of its being in the Bible."

"Of course not. It's just an allegory." She stood stiffly. What a waste of time this had been.

"Well, take another look at it. We can discuss it when you come back."

Laura turned and walked from the room without another word. What made him think she was coming back? Whenever she wanted more of his debauched philosophy she could get it in any X-rated movie for a lot less money. But then, she should have expected all this. After all, Kyle Larsen was a man. Her mother had warned her. They were all alike.

Tom was out when she got back to the room. Fine. That would give her a chance to get some writing done. Now that she was getting to know Gwendolyn better, she could do one of her character development exercises for her. Yes. Good idea.

Ten minutes later, as Laura stared at the still-blank sheet of paper in front of her, she decided that trying to write must have been a bad idea. Strange, her technique of listing everything she knew about a character, then everything she wanted to know, and then doing an imaginary talk show interview with her character never failed. But it had this time. It seemed it was taking so much energy to keep her anger at Kyle Larsen under control, she couldn't concentrate on anything else.

She wandered listlessly around the room, trying not to wonder where Tom was. The ringing phone shattered the silence that her intense concentration always created. Tom? Calling to say he was on his way? She sprang to the phone. "Hello." Silence. "Hello?"

No, not silence. Breathing. Someone was on the line, but not speaking to her.

She dropped the receiver back in the cradle with a shiver. It was as if the room had been invaded. Where was Tom? She looked around for something to do. She tried reading some of the books she had bought but couldn't focus on Canadian history. Her mind kept wandering back to Kyle Larsen's words. Slowly, amazement replaced her initial anger.

She had no idea there could be debatable theories—philosophy and theology—behind her feelings. She had been taught that things were black and white, good and evil. Now this man had said the correctness of such thoughts could be discussed. It gave a whole new approach to an issue that had been only emotion to her before.

All right, she would try his approach and see what happened. Reading the Bible couldn't hurt anything, could it? She yanked open the drawer of her bedside table and took out the Gideon Bible. Song of Solomon, he said. All right, she'd show him. She would read the whole thing, then march back into his office and tell him exactly what she and God thought of his depraved ideas. No, she wasn't going back. Well, she'd see about that.

Let him kiss me with the kisses of his mouth: for thy love is better than wine. Because of the savour of thy good ointments thy name is as ointment poured forth, therefore do the virgins love thee . . .

Tell me, O thou whom my soul loveth, where thou feedest, where thou makest thy flock to rest at noon . . . Behold, thou art fair, my beloved, yea, pleasant: also our bed is green.

Why, this was beautiful. This was the most beautiful poetry she had ever read. Why had she not seen that before? The richness of metaphor, the flow of language—Laura felt herself surrounded by warm, spiced oils, scented flowers, silken fabrics, rich foods, and the music of words carrying her on.

Who is this that cometh out of the wilderness like pillars of smoke, perfumed with myrrh and frankincense, with all powders of the merchant? Behold his bed . . .

Behold, thou art fair, my love; behold thou art fair; thou hast doves' eyes within thy locks . . . Thou art all fair, my love; there is no spot in thee . . . Thou hast ravished my heart . . . How fair is thy love . . . A garden inclosed . . . a fountain of gardens . . . Awake, O north wind; and come, thou south; blow upon my garden, that the spices thereof may flow out. Let my beloved come into his garden, and eat his pleasant fruits.

It was several moments before the knocking at the door penetrated her consciousness. Oh, it must be Tom. Had he forgotten his key? She ran to the door and flung it open as a maiden opening her garden to her lover.

The startled man in a houseboy's jacket blinked at her. "Oh, sorry to bother you. Housekeeping. Didn't realize you were in."

"But the room's been made up."

"OK. Just checking." He began to back away.

Laura frowned. Strange; housekeeping staff was usually female. She turned back to her reading, but the spell was broken. The spices and flowers were gone. Thorns and bare streambeds remained. And the serpent. There. That was the answer. She had been so seduced by the beauty of the language; she hadn't seen the serpent waiting for her. She would tell that Kyle Larsen a thing or two. Think he could deceive her, did he?

Chapter 8

"Yes, I read it just like you told me to." Laura sat in the doctor's office the next morning, her white linen blouse freshly pressed, her feet tucked carefully under her chair. "And I saw the truth you seem to have missed. Of course the garden was beautiful. But you ignored the forbidden fruit. Everyone knows the—er, the act was the forbidden fruit. That was what caused the Fall. You're telling me to enjoy the very act that brought sin into the world."

Kyle shook his head. "Theologically unsound. God commanded Adam and Even to be fruitful and multiply *before* the Fall."

Laura shrugged. "That's different. Even Augustine said having children was all right, remember?"

"Why is it different? Did God create all of the human body?"

"Yes. Of course."

"Well, then, did He create some parts good and some evil?"

Laura nibbled a fingernail. Maybe she shouldn't have come after all. She wouldn't have if she hadn't been so sure she was right on philosophical grounds. And if the all-too-familiar scenario of frustration and hostility hadn't repeated itself with Tom last night.

"You're telling me to unlearn things I've believed since I was an infant." And even as she argued, part of Laura's mind hoped he was right. How simple it would be if coming together with Tom could be in a spice-laden garden without the serpent. Simple and beautiful. And sinful.

As the apple tree among the trees of the wood, so is my beloved among the sons. I sat down under his shadow with great delight, and his fruit was sweet to my taste.

Simple and beautiful. And sinful.

Oops. The doctor was talking. And she did want to hear him. But she'd always been like this—her mind absorbed poetry like a sponge, and it was likely to wring out at odd times.

"I'm not a priest. It's not my place to tell you what to believe. But I do want you to think very carefully about some things that can make a great difference in your life. After all, it's the job of the Holy Spirit to lead us into truth—not the role of some shrink with a framed piece of paper on his wall."

He brought me to the banqueting house, and his banner over me was love.

"All right, Dr. Shrink. What do you want me to think about?" Obediently, the notebook opened to receive her lists.

"Consider the fact that God created male and female. Love—the act of love in marriage—is sacred. You and your husband were created for that relationship."

He paused until she had finished writing. "Remember that Christ pronounced the married couple to be one flesh. Sexuality is one way for a married couple to celebrate life together."

Laura drew back at the thought, but persisted, taking his words down as dictation. She numbered point three:

"The husband-wife relationship is even compared to the union between Christ and the Church. Marriage is honorable in all, and the bed undefiled."

Laura, writing fast, flipped up another sheet, ruffling the

paper. Kyle suddenly broke into laughter. "Whoa. And here I just said I wasn't a priest. Sorry about dumping all that theory on you. Tear all that up if you want to. Let's keep this simple. Write one sentence at the top of your page: Sex is a gift of God. Just that."

Laura shrank into the corner of her chair, her pen not moving.

Kyle held up a hand soothingly. "Just write it down and think about it. Work on it in your mind. Try to get comfortable with the idea."

"And what about Tom?"

"I was hoping you'd ask that. Your concern for your husband's happiness is very refreshing. Most people come in here asking, how can *I* be happier? What can *I* do to get more fulfillment for *me?* Of course, it works together—in a marriage the more satisfied one partner is the more satisfied the other will be too."

"Like what you were saying about one flesh?"

"Precisely. Try to go back to being friends with your husband before you attempt to be lovers."

"Yes. That's exactly how it used to be. Tom and I were best friends. That's what I miss so much since—since all this trouble. I've lost my best friend."

Kyle nodded. "You have to start all over on your relationship. You didn't jump into bed on your first date. Don't rush things now."

"Oh!" Laura leaned back in her chair and threw her hands up, the internal pressure escaping as if from a balloon. "Oh, it's like the first day of summer vacation."

"Good, that's just what we want. Nice and easy." He opened his desk book. "Now, I'll see you again in a week."

"A week? Oh, didn't I explain? We're only here for another week and a half. Can't I come back sooner?"

He scanned his appointments. "How about two days—Thursday morning?"

"That's perfect. Thank you so much—for everything!" Laura could never have imagined that losing an argument could be so liberating.

In her let-out-of-school spirit she chose to run down the two flights of stairs from Dr. Larsen's office rather than take the elevator. She had so much to think about. She had glimpsed a whole new world. A world ruled by a smiling, approving God. Not a thin, scowling old man holding her on a spider's web over a smoking pit hoping the filament would break. This was a whole new God. A God who created sunshine and blue skies and fields of flowers for His children to play in.

"I always feel God is watching me," she had said.

"Yes, He is," Kyle replied. "He's watching, and He approves."

"Even in bed?" It had been so hard to ask that question, to refer to the forbidden fruit in the light of day.

But Kyle had smiled at her kindly. "Especially in bed, because you're being obedient to His plan for you and your marriage."

Laura knew Kyle was right in cautioning her to go slow. It would take a long time for her subconscious to accept what her brain was saying, and then longer for her body to respond. But she had started. She had taken a step toward building a whole new structure—not just clamping down another grip on the situation with determination and willpower and clenched teeth.

This was unclenching, a letting go and relaxing. If she could really accept that God wasn't condemning her, she could quit condemning herself.

Oh, Tom, I can't wait to tell you—to start our journey back to friendship! To Laura's ecstatic vision the many-globed Victorian streetlights began to glow like iridescent opal balloons, and the baskets of trailing blossoms hanging from each lamppost nodded to her with joy.

She rounded a corner and there, leaning against one of the flower-draped lamps, was Tom, waiting for her just where he said he'd be. *Let my beloved come into his garden, and eat his pleasant fruits.* She felt as if she were running to him through a flower-strewn meadow, although in reality she somehow managed to keep both feet on the sidewalk—except for one tiny skip to match her heartbeat.

Tom stepped forward with his hands held out to meet hers, their eyes and smiles locking as warmly as their fingers. They strolled down the flower-hung street, hardly noticing the appealing shop windows or other passersby. There was so much she wanted to tell Tom, but it seemed she didn't need to. It was as if he read it all in her expression and found his own freedom in hers. Their steps hadn't matched so perfectly since their courtship days.

Tom held a door open and they entered a cozy Victorian atmosphere of dark woods and forest green carpets with etched glass on the walls and stained glass overhead. They were seated in a snug, private room. From there Laura could see into the next, a glass-roofed, plant-grown conservatory with tea drinkers seated on white wicker garden chairs. In spite of the brightness and elegance of the scene around her, though, Laura had eyes only for her husband: his firm jawline and strong chin framing fine, straight features; his crisp, white shirt collar and precise cuffs offsetting his navy blue blazer. This man was hers—her Tom. The man God had given her to become one flesh with, to live as a helpmeet with, to be friends with. *My husband, my friend.* So nonthreatening, so freeing.

Waitresses stepping out of a Victorian parlor wearing black taffeta dresses with white lace aprons and hats rustled by carrying little wicker muffin baskets. Plates of scones with Devon cream and thick strawberry preserves appeared on the lace mats in front of them. Laura reached for the white Spode teapot and filled their cups with Queen Victoria tea. She added a dollop of milk to hers and started to sip, then stopped midmotion.

There was so much she wanted to say—to explain about the past—to tell about Kyle's counseling—to promise for the future. But, almost choked with excitement, all she could get out was, "To a new beginning."

Tom's eyes, the blue-gray eyes that could be so stern, softened with the light of a smile as he reached for the handle of his yellow-flowered cup.

Laura took a bite of her flaky-yet-moist scone, then leaned back in her chair. "Mmm, afternoon tea is therapy. It nourishes the soul as well as the body. Maybe this is why Canadians are so polite."

"Americans are polite too—usually."

"Yes, but Canadians seem to give you more time with their courtesy. Small things, like calling me Mrs. James, rather than jumping into first name intimacy in a casual acquaintance."

Before Tom could reply to her sociological observations a waitress presented them with a tray of tiny finger sandwiches: delicate ham with just a hint of Dijon mustard, turkey with mayonnaise, roast beef with a suggestion of horseradish cream. The yellow buttercups blooming on Laura's plate were soon covered with delicacies. She couldn't remember when eating had ever been so much fun. She never once worried about the low-fat strictures she usually imposed.

Smiling, she piled her last bite of scone high with cream

and jam. Too high. The whole wonderful concoction slid off halfway between plate and mouth, streaking the front of her blouse. "Oh, no. What a place to be a klutz." She scrubbed vigorously with her linen napkin.

"That's OK. They'll just put it down to the fact that you're an American."

"Right. More casual and relaxed."

"You really are, aren't you?" Tom sounded so encouraging, his candid question was the perfect opening for Laura.

"Oh, yes. Can you tell already?"

"I could tell when I saw you half a block away. You look about five years younger. And—it's funny, but you look taller."

"Tom, that's a perfect observation. It's because I'm not afraid to stand up straight."

"What?"

"Well, at this point I'm still telling myself I don't need to be afraid, but I'll have it internalized soon."

"Explain."

"Well, I guess the most astonishing thing I learned was that the devil didn't make sex; God did." And she even said the word right out, without so much as gulping first or blushing after.

Tom continued munching sandwiches, but he leaned toward her, wearing the slight frown that always meant he was concentrating. At last he shook his head. "Laura, I never knew. I just thought you didn't like me. Why didn't you ever *say* anything?"

"Because I never had any idea I was any different. Oh, different from popular stuff on TV and the terrible things you read in the paper—and thank goodness. But I thought all *nice* women felt the way I did."

The waitress held the pastry tray in front of them with

maybe a dozen kinds of enticing confections. "Oh, how can I choose?" Laura groaned.

"You can have two if you want—or more," the waitress offered.

Laura looked at Tom and laughed. "You may have to roll me out of here, but I'm going to do it. This one and that one, and—" She hesitated, and before she could settle the issue with her conscience the waitress added a mocha almond truffle to the collection on her plate.

"I don't know what's come over me." Laura laughed at Tom's amazed expression. "I haven't abandoned all restraint like this since . . . since . . . Well, I must have let myself go sometime before."

"I don't think so. If this is the new Laura, I think I'm going to love being married to her."

"All 300 pounds of her?"

"Maybe we can find some other way to channel her released inhibitions before that happens."

The pastries were so rich that Laura left the milk out of her tea to help them go down. "I'm glad we're not flying out tonight on that bouncy airplane."

They were laughing together over that awful experience when the waitress brought long-stemmed dishes of creamy white syllabub topped with chocolate-dipped strawberries. Laura took a spoonful of the tangy, light pudding. "So that's what it tastes like. I've always wondered. Jane Austen's characters ate gallons of syllabub—not all at one time, of course."

And then the bill came—topped with tiny mousse-filled chocolate cups—which, of course, had to be eaten before the bill could be paid. Laura poured the last few drops of tea. "Time to quit. The pot's empty. Now let's go work this orgy off by shopping."

"Uh-ho, when you get that gleam in your eye I'm in trouble."

"You aren't, but your pocketbook is!" Laura took her friend's arm and they started their survey of the shops: Scottish tartans, English China, Canadian furs and ivory . . . "This looks like a good place to buy some gifts." Laura indicated a shop displaying an abundance of maple leafs and union jacks. Even though the queen no longer signed Canadian bills into law, it was obvious the people carried a dual loyalty in their hearts. "Have you noticed how they put up pictures of the royal family everywhere—like most people put up pictures of their favorite aunts and uncles." Suddenly every detail took on new meaning because she could share it with her friend.

Laura selected demitasse spoons, one decorated with a figure of Queen Victoria and another with enameled white dogwood blossoms—the provincial flower. Tom joined her at the cash register. "See what I found for Phil." He held out a finely etched piece of scrimshaw.

"Great! That'll be perfect on his desk. And what a beautiful plate—your mother will love it."

Tom started to reply, but the clerk held out a pen. "If you will please be so kind as to sign right here, Mr. James."

They drifted on up the street. "Oh, look. A whole shop of Crabtree & Evelyn products. Let's go smell their soaps. You could get a gift for your sister here."

Half an hour later, with Laura carrying a bag smelling like a country garden, they went on to Trounce Alley with its historic shops dating from the gold rush days.

"It's about closing time. What else do you have on your list?" Tom asked as they left a shop of Australian and New Zealand imports.

Laura consulted her notes. "Roger's Chocolates, home of

fine Victorian creams since 1885."

"Don't tell me you're hungry already?"

"I don't think I'll ever be hungry again. But I'm told you can't come to Victoria without buying Roger's chocolates. I don't think they let you through customs without them."

"Yeah, the officials probably confiscate them and eat them themselves."

They entered the rich atmosphere of dark oak paneling, tartan wallpaper, stained glass, and red-lighted art nouveau lamps. "Oh, just *breathe!*" Laura followed her own command. "I wonder how many calories one takes in simply breathing in here?"

They crossed the marble floor to the high oak counter. Tom chose the flavors: cherry, mint, peach, vanilla nut . . . As he named them a girl plopped chocolate creams the size of baking powder biscuits, wrapped in shiny red and gold foil, into a bag.

It was getting dark by the time they emerged again into the sea-scented evening air. "Look," Laura pointed. "The Parliament Building is lit. Let's walk around the harbor."

The last pale tinges of the sunset faded as they strolled along the Waterfront Promenade. The ivy-covered stone walls of the Empress looked even more castlelike when aglow with lights. Laura looked up to the green-roofed gables and turrets. "The rooms with those tiny windows way up there—those must be the garrets where the dollar ladies lived. Can't you just imagine them bravely making the best of the situation, declaring the view to be much improved in their new rooms while they brewed reused tea leaves."

And then the cathedral-shaped Parliament Buildings came into view with their etching of thousands of amber lights. Laura stopped. "Can you believe that's real? I mean—not real at Disneyland or something—but a real government building, where real laws are made."

"Makes you think of something Eastern—like Scheherazade or the Taj Mahal, doesn't it?"

"Exactly. And here it is, an offspring of the Mother of Parliaments."

"Can you imagine replacing those lightbulbs?" Tom shook his head.

"I read an article about it. Some of the original carbon filament lights were still functioning when they did extensive restoration a few years ago."

They continued their stroll, admiring the building and the lights reflected in the harbor. "The architect was a genius. Same fellow who designed the Empress, wasn't it?" Tom asked.

"Yes, and the Crystal Gardens and the Bank of Montreal. What would Victoria be without Rattenbury? But I think the Parliament was the first—at least he did it before the Empress. I read that he was only 25 years old when he won the design competition. Later he went back to England and married a young wife. She and her lover poisoned him. The murder trial was a sensation."

Tom laughed. "What an amazing storehouse of information you are!"

Laura considered pointing out that in spite of his complaints, traveling with a compulsive researcher could have advantages; but things were going too well to take any chances on raising a controversy.

They paused before a statue of Queen Victoria. Laura started to comment on its enormous size when she caught her breath. It had only been a quick movement in the dark, but she was sure. Almost. "There's someone hiding behind the statue," she whispered.

They backed away, then circled wide around the huge

sculpture. When they reached the back, three large, loud sea-gulls squawked away with an indignant flapping of wings.

Laura laughed. "See, what did I tell you? Lurking to nab our chocolates, they were."

Tom's arm was warm and strong under her hand, and they strolled so slowly she could have rested her head on his shoulder. *A perfect day is one in which you've made a new friend,* Laura recalled from somewhere—probably a greeting card. She squeezed Tom's arm.

The Empress welcomed the strollers with her gracious charm. They entered the elevator and smiled at each other with amused amazement when a lady joined them—bringing her bicycle with her.

"I suppose the Empress has seen everything in her life-time," Tom said when they got off.

Laura grinned up at him. "That's what makes her a great lady—she never flutters."

Tom held the heavy door to their room open and Laura entered, dropped her packages, and sank down on the floral love seat. "Oh, why didn't I bring my tennie runners?" She kicked off her medium-heeled pumps.

"Because you never remember to take your tennis shoes anywhere." Tom knelt in front of her and began massaging her tired feet.

"M-m-m, clever plan, huh? If my feet didn't hurt, you wouldn't rub them for me."

Tom massaged the balls of her feet, the arches, the back of her heels. Laura slid deeper into the settee, her whole body relaxing to his touch. Then his fingers made their way up her leg. When they reached the sensitive spot inside her knee, she jerked. The response her action brought to Tom's eyes was not one of pleasure. "I'm sorry." She giggled to cover her tension. "It tickled."

"That's OK." Tom stood up. "I need to call Phil before we get carried away."

"At this hour?"

"He needs some figures for a meeting in the morning. I couldn't get hold of him before we met for tea. You run along to bed. Hopefully this won't take too long."

A few minutes later Laura was in bed, bits of Tom's business conversation carrying in to her from the other room. She reached for her journal: *One of the best days of my life! Beginning a whole new chapter: Friendship with Tom.*

She chewed the end of her pen for a moment. *Goals: cultivate companionship; nourish our relationship. I'll get my horticultural degree in love-growing. Love doesn't come like a bush of full-blown roses; it doesn't stay in bloom without feeding, pruning, protecting. Like everything else that's alive, it must be kept growing through care or it will wilt away. The aphids, blackspot, and mildew almost won, but now they're on the run . . .*

Tom gently removed the pen and book from her hands and placed himself there instead. She happily, freely returned his kisses and caresses. This was so wonderful, so right. It had been so long since their love had been nurtured with such simple affection.

Then everything changed. Tom drew closer to her. Suddenly Laura's whole body stiffened. A sob of protest caught in her throat. Her fingers dug into his shoulders as she pushed him away. What was happening? Hadn't she explained about the friendship part? It was supposed to be like when they were just dating, when going beyond kissing wasn't a consideration. Didn't he understand?

She didn't have to push hard. Tom was out of bed in a single jump. He turned back to her in cold fury. "What kind of a put-on is this? Everything was just hunky-dory all day until it comes to the big test. But nothing's really changed, has it? All those great platitudes about love and friendship that quack fed you—they don't mean a thing when it comes to putting up or shutting up."

"Tom! I'm sorry!" She clutched the comforter, pulling it to her chin. "I didn't mean to do that. Honest. I couldn't help it. It wasn't even you I was pushing away. I—I—I don't know. I wasn't even in this room. It sounds crazy, but it was all dark, and I heard kids talking and spoons rattling and—like in a cafeteria or something—Tom! Don't look at me that way! I'm not making this up!" She tried to go on but choked. "Tom, please, can't we take Kyle's advice and just be friends? Just for a start? It will work. I know it will. Please."

"*Friends.* A fine excuse to keep me on a leash while you keep your prudish, virginal distance. Sure, just friends. I'll carry your books home from school, and you can share your jelly beans with me. No thanks. I outgrew jelly beans in the sixth grade." He yanked the quilted spread off the foot of the bed, grabbed a pillow, and stalked into the sitting room.

Chapter 9

Long into the night Laura lay curled in the middle of the bed, a tight ball of misery. *I thought it was solved. I really did. Not all finished, but the first, right steps. Enough to make a difference. O God, what next? What else is there? I was so sure, but it went so wrong. What can I do?*

But when she listened for an answer, it wasn't the voice of God she heard. It was the voice of her mother. Not the gentle, loving voice of a nursery-picture mother, but her mother, turning on her and snarling like a cat. "That did *not* happen, and don't you ever talk about it again! I'll not have you making up disgusting lies like that."

And then it all flooded back.

The pictures filled her mind, holding her in a nightmare. But this was no figment of a creative subconscious. It was a clear, vivid memory, as sharp and painful as the moment it happened. She lay still, barely breathing. She wanted to turn away, to smash the awful scenes like a mirror. But it wasn't a mirror. It was herself.

At last it ended and she could breathe. She could move. She flung out of bed. In her rush to get to Tom she almost fell down the steps from the bedroom. "Tom! Tom, I've just remembered. Wake up." She knelt by his sprawled form in the middle of the floor and shook his shoulder. "Wake up, I've got to tell you. I had completely for-gotten—for years and years. It just came back! Tom, listen to me."

Tom leaned up on one elbow and shook his head to clear it.

"I was in the seventh grade. We had this special teacher for drama that came two or three times a week and taught us Christmas plays and stuff. I loved drama. I always got the best parts. I thought Mr. Sanders was wonderful. He was even a friend of my mother's. He used to come visit. It made me feel special."

"Sort of a father figure?"

"No!" She pulled back at the very idea. "But almost an uncle. I guess—I never had an uncle, either." She paused. "Anyway, we were getting some things ready for a drama festival. I was doing a dramatic monologue—some really psychological thing about a woman going crazy in a room with yellow wallpaper. I was having trouble with it, so Mr. Sanders asked me to stay backstage one noon hour for a special rehearsal.

"As soon as we were alone, he started hugging me and kissing me. He put his hand up under my sweater . . . I wanted to cry out, but I was too frightened to make a sound. The floor was so hard. He was so heavy. I was so scared someone would come in. What would they think? I kept listening for footsteps, but all I could hear was the kids in the cafeteria.

"Then it was over. I was so confused. I didn't know what had happened or how to act. So I said, 'I think I should go now.' And he let me go. Only first he asked me not to tell anyone what he'd done.

"I guess I thought I wouldn't, but I was frightened and mixed up and the pressure just kept building up inside. I wanted to cry. I couldn't eat. Finally I told my mother that night."

"And?"

"And she said it didn't happen. She said I was a wicked,

evil girl to make up a story like that. And if Mr. Sanders touched me at all, it was because I behaved like a brazen hussy."

"What!" Tom jerked fully upright.

Suddenly Laura realized what she'd done. She clamped both hands over her mouth to choke back a sob. Horror filled her eyes. She had told. She'd told Tom. Now he would know her secret—the awful truth about her. Now he would hate her like her mother did.

"I'm sorry. I shouldn't have told. I—I didn't think . . ." She stuck her fingers in her mouth and backed away.

"Laura, wait. We need to talk."

Talk? Tom wanted to talk? He wasn't too disgusted with her? She sat on the edge of a chair, her bare feet tucked far back.

"How could a mother react like that?" His words amazed her. He wanted to know about her mother? He wasn't asking her how she could have done such an awful thing?

"I—I don't know. I never thought about her."

"And how did you feel?"

"I believed what she said. Not that it didn't happen, but that it was my fault. That I was bad."

"So you've kept it buried all these years just as if it didn't happen." He was quiet for a moment. "Laura, that must have been awful for you."

A shudder ran through her body. "Yes, it was." She scrubbed at her mouth with the back of her hand. "His lips were wet. His hands were sweaty. The whole room seemed slimy." She covered her face with her hands. "I need a bath."

Tom put a hand on her shoulder. "Laura, you're shivering. You don't need a bath. You aren't dirty. Not on the inside or the outside. Come to bed and get warm." He picked up the bedspread.

She looked at him with wide eyes, trying not to shrink from his suggestion.

"Laura, you have my word; I won't touch you. But we both need to sleep. Come on, we'll talk more in the morning."

Tom yawned once, turned on his side, and began snoring softly. But Laura wasn't sleepy. She felt an almost overwhelming compulsion to cry, and yet she remained dry-eyed. The weeping was going on inside her. Weeping for the years of fear and hurt a little girl had carried. Weeping for the scars that covered all the pent-up misery and self-hatred. Slowly the frozen grief she bore thawed and flooded her in an emotional washing.

She snuggled close to Tom, savoring the warmth his sleeping body radiated. "I'm going to get better, Tom. Truly I am. Then you can really love me."

Laura was up early the next morning, anxious to tell Kyle of her progress. Surely it was progress—even if she had had to regress to get there.

She smoothed her crisp brown hair and turned to slip on her tailored jacket when the phone rang. She would grab it before it woke Tom. "Hello."

The silence was punctuated with a sharp click.

Laura froze. One or two such calls one could chalk up to misdirections. But this was three now. Not a dead line, but someone there. Someone there but silent. Who could it be but Marla? Marla calling for Tom.

Laura turned woodenly to keep her appointment, wondering what use it was. Was there enough of a marriage left to attempt a rescue?

". . . Was your parents' marriage happy?" Today Kyle remained seated behind his desk while Laura sat in an upholstered armchair beside it.

"My parents? I have no idea. My father died in a car wreck before I was born. Mother never talked about him at all. Why?"

"Because the marital pain of the parents can capture the children, deprive them of the freedom to experience growth and joy in intimacy. The account you've just shared with me of your mother's reaction to your molestation makes me suspect there were problems there."

Laura gave a brittle little laugh. "I can't imagine my mother ever being intimate with *anyone*. The very thought's enough to make me wonder how I got here at all."

Kyle nodded and bounced his pencil eraser on his desk. "You see, our parenting roles and our intimacy skills are largely derived from the model our parents provided."

"Then it's no wonder I don't possess any."

"On the contrary; it's a wonder you possess as many as you do. You and Tom seem to have a very good relationship in many ways."

Laura shrugged. "I read a lot. But Jane Austen and Charlotte Brontë can only teach you so much. Especially since neither of them ever married."

"Not only do you lack the role model, but subconsciously you may fear that achieving true intimacy with your husband would risk your mother's anger, rejection, and jealousy."

"I don't know about jealousy, but it never took much to rouse her anger or rejection."

"What did your mother teach you about life?"

Laura thought for a moment. "She taught me that humankind is sinful. That we have to work hard to overcome our basic evil instincts—the sex drive being number one on the list.

" 'Fear God. Fear God; you do something wrong and

He'll wash you away in the flood.' " Laura gasped. "That's what she said, but I hadn't thought of it for years."

"And did she give you any sex education?"

Laura gave a brittle laugh. "Aside from what Mr. Sanders taught me, I learned the 'facts of life' when I was a freshman in high school: If you kiss a boy, you get pregnant."

"She said that? Surely your friends would have given you a different slant on the matter?"

"I didn't have any friends close enough to talk to about such things. Tom was my first close friend." She closed her eyes and wrinkled her brow with the effort to recall what her mother had said. "I guess that was just my general impression of things. Her precise information was, 'You know how boys are made. You know how girls are made. Well, put two and two together.' "

Laura slumped back in her chair, exhausted with the effort of remembering. Kyle sat quietly until at last she sighed and looked up. "Laura, I know this is going to be hard for you—very hard, but you must confront your mother about these feelings you're carrying."

Laura started to protest, but Kyle went on. "A barrier to intimacy with a parent will also be a barrier to intimacy with a spouse. You must learn to relate as a responsible adult to your mother as a first step toward reaching your husband. You've got to deal with these old hurts and fears in order to bring them to closure and remove them as barriers to your fulfillment."

Laura shook her head, feeling dazed. Today her notebook stayed closed. She could barely manage to listen to this, much less write it down.

Kyle smiled. "It's a long road, Laura. You've got a lot of work to do—years maybe. I know I'm throwing an awful lot of psychological jargon at you, but I want to give you as much scientific basis for understanding the situation as possible. And I want you to see that the goal at the end is worth the effort."

Laura nodded. "Tom."

Kyle shook his head. "Tom *and* you. Together. A real marriage. A real life. I told you last time you had to start your relationship with Tom over anew. Today I'm telling you to go back a lot farther than that. We psychiatrists often wish human emotions were as precise as mathematical formulas— it'd make our job a lot easier. But people do follow certain patterns of development. What happens when a parent doesn't affirm a child's development is that the child's self-esteem will be deficient. You will have to rebuild your image of self-worth through the affirmation of your husband and through your Heavenly Father."

Laura winced. Did he have to use that term? But she answered calmly, "Yes, I can understand that. Mother demanded so much perfection I could never make the grade. A's were never good enough. They had to be A pluses. And since there was just Mother and me in our family, I had no other standard to judge myself by." Then Laura's expression tightened. She looked at Kyle with fear in her eyes. "Surely it's enough if I understand this and talk to Tom about it. I can't talk to my mother about *sex*."

Kyle regarded her levelly. "Do you want to be free to love your husband?"

"Of course I do."

"Then you must forgive your mother."

Laura just looked at him. Her eyes and mouth were wide open, but no words came out.

Chapter 10

Forgive your mother. Forgive your mother. The phrase rang over and over in Laura's head like a knell as she drove across the island to meet Glenda at Oak Bay.

I had no idea I blamed her for anything. I thought everything was my fault. But now that I see it—now that I remember and really understand what she did—that's an awful lot to forgive.

How could you do that, Mother? How could you say those things? You've practically ruined my life. And I'm supposed to forgive you? Just like that? I don't know how you could have done what you did. And I don't know how I'm going to do what I've got to do.

She continued talking out loud to her mother, shouting even, in the little car. Somehow, just saying the words helped. She pretended her mother was beside her in the passenger seat. *Didn't you care? How did you think I felt? Why, why, why? Did being mean to me make you feel good? Did it give you a sense of power, knowing you were ruining my life? Were you in love with Mr. Sanders? Were you jealous because he chose me instead of you?*

She quieted as she drove into the tiny English village atmosphere of Oak Bay. She decided she would simply do her best to put the whole thing out of her mind and enjoy her time with Glenda. After all, it had been out of her mind—the conscious part, at least—for 17 years. A few more hours wouldn't hurt anything.

She pulled into a parking spot right on the corner Glenda

had appointed as a meeting place. And there she was. "Incredible!" Glenda greeted her. "Are you always so prompt?"

"Well, you know, the Lord takes care of idiots and newcomers—so I get a double dose of help."

Glenda laughed and led the way into the cozy Scottish atmosphere of The Blethering Place. Nothing could have been more comforting after Laura's frazzling morning than the fresh-baked bread aroma, old lace curtains, and soft Tiffany lights filling the busy tea shop. The women found a quiet corner by a small-paned window, and Laura ordered one of the enormous Scottish cheese scones she saw others devouring around her. Their copious teapot came swathed in a colorful woolen cozy.

"Oh, I love this. If only I could knit." Laura played with the saucy round yarn pom-pom atop their pink and brown pot cover.

"No need. The local ladies make skeeds of these woollies. They have drawers full of them in the foyer—all for sale."

"Wonderful! That should just finish my gift shopping for my writers' group. Of course, I'll have to explain them. They'll think I'm giving them ski caps." It wasn't until Glenda reached for the blue and white sugar bowl in the center of the table that Laura noticed her friend's hand was trembling. "Glenda! What's the matter?"

"Nothing new, I suppose. Nothing really different. But that's the problem. Kyle counsels and I prune roses and we see each other two or three times a week and I dream of him every night. And I'm going crazy."

"Glenda, have you talked to him about this? Kyle Larsen is the world's easiest person to talk to—believe me, I know. I've been doing it by the hour."

Glenda sighed. "Last night I was determined I would. I'd

gone through everything in my head about six times. I went to his house, and we sat around all relaxed and toasted muffins by the fire. It couldn't have been more perfect. Then Darren's school counselor called and said Darren had been truant that day, and two of his friends had been picked up for shoplifting."

"And Darren?"

"He wasn't with them, apparently. But Kyle was upset about the truancy. It hardly made a good opportunity for me to plead my case."

"Yes, I can see that." Laura took a long, thoughtful sip of tea. "What you need is Kyle's undivided attention like I get in his office."

"I know. I've often wished I were his patient rather than his girlfriend. His patients get far more of his time than I do."

"Glenda! That's it!"

"What is?"

"He does premarital counseling, too, doesn't he?"

"Sure. He says if he could see more couples before marriage it would save years of counseling later."

"Then make an appointment with him."

"Me?"

"Sure, give a nom de plume, say you and your boyfriend are having problems and you feel you need his professional help."

Glenda giggled. "Can you imagine the look on his face when I walk in. What name shall I give?"

"How about Gwendolyn?"

"A lovely name, but why that?"

"Name of my heroine."

"The one who grows roses? Perfect! Do you think I can disguise my voice enough?"

"Can't you just talk to the receptionist?"

"Kyle prefers to make his own appointments. But I think I can pull it off. Oh, I feel so much better! Come on, let's go shopping to celebrate!"

"I've done most of the tourist spots. Show me where you really shop."

Since Glenda had gone to Oak Bay by bus, they drove back downtown in Laura's car. "There's a dress shop right up here on Douglas Street. Enough racks to keep us busy for hours. Good styles and working girl prices."

The trim saleslady in a proper black dress and pearls asked if she could help. Glenda replied that they were just browsing. "Well, you just carry on then, my dears."

And that is precisely what they did: through stacks of sweaters, racks of lingerie, tables of hats. Laura hadn't felt so much like a schoolgirl, or a little girl dressing up in her mother's clothes, for years and years. At home she did almost all her shopping from the myriad of direct mail catalogs that filled her mailbox and required her spending none of her time in the malls. It was an efficient method and the results were highly satisfactory for the turtlenecks and blazers she preferred. But a shopping spree with a friend filled an entirely different need from merely stocking her wardrobe with the basics.

"Laura, just come see this gorgeous thing!"

Laura looked at the shimmering scarlet silk caftan Glenda was holding out. "Oh, try it on!" Laura urged.

"Not me, silly. It's made for you. Come on."

Laura held back. She had never in her life even looked at anything so seductively alluring as this garment. "I, uh—I don't think that's quite me."

"Maybe not the you you are. But how about the you you'd like to be?"

Laura laughed. "You sound like you've been talking to a

psychiatrist. What was it Kyle said, 'It's never hypocrisy to act the way you'd like to feel'?"

"Sure. Didn't you ever want to feel sexy?"

Laura pushed aside her instinct to draw back. She forced herself to touch the soft, clingy fabric. She looked at the low neckline without blinking. "Well . . ."

"Come on. It'll knock Tom's eyes out."

"Is that what I want to do?"

"Of course it is."

"OK then, practice what you preach—let's find something for you to wear to your appointment with Dr. Larsen."

"Wait a minute. I'm a gardener, not a romance writer. I'm an outdoors girl—cutoffs and straw hats."

"Which is precisely why this blouse will get his attention." Laura held out a black crepe, dolman sleeved blouse embroidered with peacock-colored beads. "Do you have a skirt to go with this?"

Glenda admitted that she did. A short time later the two women, looking cat-with-the-creamish, emerged from the shop with their bundles. "Let's go to the English Sweet Shop and get something to take to our fellas," Glenda said.

"I thought that's what we just did."

"Yeah, you're right. But why hold back once we've started? Besides, I've got a fatal weakness for their English Mix."

So they added small white bags of chocolates from Brussels, mints from South Africa, and toffee from England to their day's hoard before Laura walked Glenda to her bus stop. "Let me know how it all goes," Laura said.

"Don't worry, I couldn't keep it. It feels so good just to have some sort of a plan! Why don't you and Tom go to church with us Sunday? We might be able to get in a bit of a private word then."

Church? How long had it been since she and Tom had gone to church together? "Well—sure. Why not? I'll ask Tom."

On the way back to the Empress, Laura eyed the bag containing the red caftan as uneasily as if it were a living thing. What had she done? In her mind she saw herself standing before the dressing room mirror, the lights overhead making the fabric dazzle. She gasped again at the remembered sight her contours revealed so—so—well, so revealingly under the flowing fabric. Just the color alone made her think of Rahab the harlot and her scarlet thread.

Guilt and shame overcame her for purchasing such a thing. She signaled a left-hand turn. She would go around the block here and take it right back to the store. How could she have been so wanton? What would Tom think if he had seen her in that thing? He would have thought her mother was right about her enticing that man to misbehave. Maybe her mother was right. If she could buy a thing like this to entice Tom, maybe she had done something like that as a child and then repressed the memory.

A horn blared behind her. She jumped and realized the light had changed. She rounded the corner and pulled into a parking spot. But before she even turned her engine off, the image of Kyle Larsen rose before her, sitting across from her, tapping the eraser end of his pencil on his desk.

"Does it help you to know you're not alone in your feelings? Identifying sex with guilt is not at all uncommon. The Bible so often speaks against the misuses of sex—such as adultery or fornication—that many people have concluded erroneously that God condemns all sex. But remember, He's the one who created men and women to complement each other physically. Have you got that—not opposites. Complements."

"Yes, but—"

105

"And then, of course, there are some people who believe that anything that pleases God can't be fun . . ."

Laura thought for a moment. "No, I don't believe that. A God who created roses couldn't be dour."

"That's right. And He wants you to find even greater joy in your marriage than you do in your rose garden."

"I do enjoy part of it—being held close, feelings of tenderness . . ."

"Right. That's exactly the right place to start. Concentrate on that. Then go on to concentrate on the joy of giving your husband pleasure. Forget about yourself. It's thoughts of yourself that are inhibiting you—not thoughts of Tom."

"But what if I don't make him happy? I don't think I could stand another failure."

Kyle's pencil tapped. "I don't think you need to worry about that. Nothing satisfies a man like knowing he has satisfied his wife. If you're happy, he'll be happy."

"Yes! Tom told me that once, but I couldn't cope with it at the time." She paused. "And if I'm unhappy, he's unhappy. I guess that's what's called a vicious cycle."

"Nothing could be further from vicious when it's going the right direction. When your husband is convinced that you love him for himself and enjoy his lovemaking, he'll become more confident in all areas of his life and be a better husband—in or out of bed."

The full implication of that concept overwhelmed Laura. She tried to imagine how wonderful life could be with that principle in operation in their home. Laura felt an incredible joy, like a new birth. She was more than prepared to die to her old inhibitions, her old self-consciousness. *I'll be born a new and better self in real communion with Tom. I'll . . .*

Another blaring horn made Laura jump and brought her back sharply to the real world. The real world of automobiles and city traffic. She eased out into the street and drove to the hotel, the scarlet caftan still on the seat beside her.

Tom met her at the door of their room. "Where have you been? I thought we had a date to go to the castle this afternoon."

"Oh, Tom, I'm sorry! How could I have forgotten?" She knew how he hated to be kept waiting. And here he'd been, getting more and more frustrated while she daydreamed about how happy she would make him.

Chapter 11

"Is it too late to go now?"

Tom glanced at his watch. "Probably not. If you're sure you can fit me into your schedule."

"I said I'm sorry. I know I should have called when Glenda and I decided to go shopping, but I guess I thought you'd be so involved in your work you'd be glad not to be interrupted."

"*If* you thought at all."

She dropped her packages on the bed and followed Tom into the hall. "How is Phil getting along at the office?"

"K.C. looks better than ever." Tom glowed with excitement. "I may even press for a whole percentage point more. If our backer will just stay with us until it's signed, Marsden and James, Inc. should be financially independent at last."

Laura nodded just as if she understood the machinations of his business activities. But one thing she understood—getting him talking about the world of high finance and investment properties would take his mind off his irritation with her.

She listened with one ear as she reached for her briefcase and pulled out her guidebook notes on the building they were to visit. Craigdarroch Castle was built a hundred years ago by Robert Dunsmuir who promised his young wife that if she would accompany him to Victoria from Scotland he would "become rich and build her a castle with a porte cochere and liveried coachmen and she would give grand dinner parties under crystal chandeliers."

Her mind full of this prince-in-shining-armor vision, Laura's consciousness came back to Tom's words, ". . . and of course, eliminating the middleman on that stage of the procedure will give us more margin for profit for ourselves or for reducing fees to the consumer . . ."

"I'm sorry. I missed that part. How will you cut out a middleman?"

"By having the contractor be his own investor—then we won't have to borrow capital from an outside lender . . ."

Laura really did try to follow his explanations, but then her eye caught the story of the wedding of the Dunsmuirs' daughter: "The most fashionable and brilliant ever witnessed in Victoria. The bride's gown was white and silver brocade with full court train, brocaded in silver in the pattern of the Prince of Wales' crest. The wedding party included six bridesmaids, several trainbearers and flower girls, and 20 friends of the bride as maids of honor. The bride and bridegroom received some 300 guests at Craigdarroch, the fashionable company spending several merry hours in the palatial residence and its beautiful gardens while the band of the HMS *Warspite* played . . ."

". . . But then if this falls through, I don't really know what we'll do. Phil's age and health don't make heavy indebtedness sensible for the company, and I—"

"Tom!" His words suddenly made sense. "Are you saying we're in financial trouble?"

"No, I'm not saying that at all. I'm saying we need this Kansas City deal to be really independent."

"You do expect to get it, don't you?"

"You never have a deal until the money's changed hands. But it looks good."

"Well, then, let's quit worrying." And as if worries could disappear and castles appear magically, Craigdarroch, a sugarplum fairy confection of steep red-roofed gables, conical turrets, and multiple chimneys rose before them. Laura resisted the urge to take out her notebook. *You're not here for research. You're here to give Tom pleasure. To be with him.*

They entered the mellow wood-paneled grand hall and went on to a music room where intricately jeweled stained-glass windows brought splashes of color to the ornate white and gold walls under a rain forest of crystal chandeliers— Robert Dunsmuir had been a man of his word. All the light and color was reflected and rereflected in equally ornate mirrors adorning the walls on every side of the room. Laura laughed and started to wave to their repeated images when she stopped. Was that tall, redheaded fellow with acne staring at her? She turned, but he was gone. Silly of her. He was just looking at the marvelous mirror—like all the other tourists. Or admiring his earring in it.

And then Laura's attention moved to a white alabaster statue of a bonneted baby girl lying on her stomach, playing. Subconsciously Laura's hand went to her flat abdomen.

She turned at the guide's words and made herself focus on the unique fireplaces with flues that divided around stained-glass windows centered over the mantels in the library and dining room. They moved on to the carriage entrance: the promised porte cochere. Apparently the Scottish prince charming had fulfilled all his promises. Laura moved ahead of Tom into the central entry, rich with multiple varieties of wood. She held on to the railing so she could look straight up through four floors of curving oak banisters and brass chandeliers.

The wooden floor creaked sharply behind her. She turned but was dizzy from looking up. When her head cleared, no one was there. She was still puzzling over the small incident when Tom joined her. They went on from room to room,

Laura becoming increasingly entranced with the pictures on the walls—not the prized oil paintings written up in the guidebooks but the simple, black-and-white pictures of children. The first one to capture her attention was an Edwardian photograph of Julie, eight-year-old granddaughter of the Dunsmuirs, in a low-waisted white dress with a big hair ribbon, holding up a skirt full of blossoms while dropping a single rose behind her. Then to the nursery, its walls covered with delightful old lithographs of children playing blindman's bluff in a flower-filled garden, golden-haired children at a picnic tea along a riverbank, laughing children playing tug-of-war with their grandfather . . .

"Victorian sentimentality." Tom shook his head.

Yanked out of her personal yearnings, Laura realized how little she had succeeded in connecting emotionally with Tom on this excursion. "I think it's rather wonderful." She turned back down the stairs.

"And apparently so did your friend, as absorbed as he seemed to be in every item." Tom crunched across the parking lot to the car with long strides.

"My friend? What are you talking about?"

"Your friend from the museum. Don't try to tell me you didn't see him. I saw you start to wave to him in the mirror before you saw me looking. Who did you say you had tea with today?"

"You know perfectly well I was with Glenda. If that man—whoever he is—was here—and, no, I didn't see him—it was just a coincidence. Why are you so fixated about this?"

"Some masher is following my wife around, and *I'm* the one who's fixated?"

Laura remained quiet. Aggravating as the exchange was, she couldn't help being pleased that Tom cared enough to be jealous. And besides, she could tell by the look on Tom's face that he was back to running calculations in his head again. Any incident at Craigdarroch—real or imagined—was forgotten.

Well, the day wasn't over—or at least the night. She could still hope to get his attention at a quiet, candlelight dinner. She had looked up several choices in the guidebook. "Tom, this evening—"

"Yeah, I was going to talk to you about that. I need to get back to Phil in the morning with some final figures on the K.C. property. Do you mind if we have dinner in our room rather than going out?"

"Oh, no, I don't mind at all." So much for a warmly romantic dinner to ease her into the mood to wear that caftan tonight. But then, it would be the perfect apparel for a candlelight dinner in the room. Of course, the purpose of this dinner was to give Tom more time to punch out figures on his supermeg laptop. Still, maybe she could arrange something.

Back in their room, Laura stifled a sigh, picked up a copy of *Writer's Digest*, and curled into a corner of the love seat. She looked across the room at the small jade green fireplace and wished, as she did every time she looked at it, that it weren't just for decoration; there was nothing like dancing flames and glowing embers to improve the atmosphere. She thumbed through her magazine, pausing to read interviews with two of her favorite romance writers, scored well on the Grammar Grappler, and read the fiction column—all to the accompaniment of her growling stomach. Finally their room service order arrived.

Tom didn't actually bring his laptop to the table with him, but he might as well have. Laura could see the figures calculating in his mind. Immediately after dinner he went back to his charts. And Laura went back to her place alone on the love seat. *Honeymoon. Right.*

Well, since Tom was spending the evening on math, so would she. Opening her briefcase she took out the neatly columned business-expense-tracker Tom had designed for her. Well, he had really designed it for himself since he did the bookkeeping, but it was for her to fill in the blanks. After scrabbling in coat pockets, purse, sacks, and the odd corner for receipts and jotted notes, Laura transferred all the figures to neat columns. The columns were neat, even if her figures weren't. The only thing she liked about that job was that she felt positively righteous when it was finished.

From the appearance of Tom's head bent over his work, Laura knew it was going to be a long evening. But she always had her own refuge. She pulled out her notebook.

"Kevin, I love you so much." Gwendolyn clung to him and sobbed. "Why won't you let me share your life—your joys and your sorrows?"

"When someone promises to take me for better or for worse, I want them to have at least even odds of getting the better." He shook her hand off his arm and . . .

"How's it going?"

Laura was so lost in the pictures in her head she jumped visibly when Tom spoke to her. "Oh, hello. Well, it's getting nicely complicated. The hero's younger brother is involved with a group of hoodlums . . ."

"I thought you were writing a romance, not a thriller."

"Category romances are getting more realistic. Readers are getting tired of all that fantasy stuff."

"Hmmm. Well, I suppose troubled teens are realistic." Tom shrugged and returned to his papers.

And so is a troubled marriage. Laura forced her mind back to her work. It worried her not to know where her story was really going. She usually had it all worked out before taking a research trip; that avoided wasting precious travel time. But when she returned to the blank paper in front of her, it was her own thoughts that filled her head, not her heroine's.

Kyle said today that intimacy has its own inner law—it must either grow or die. It looks like our patient needs a transfusion. Would appearing before Tom in that caftan be a cure? Or a fatal shock? But the question isn't what it will do to Tom. What will it do to me?

The picture in her mind was of herself in the scarlet robe, standing below a towering wall she must cross to get to Tom. The enormous, hand-hewn stones were labeled: fear, distrust, self-consciousness . . . All the barriers her early training had erected loomed around her. Did she want to remove that wall, even if she could? The same wall that hemmed one in could also keep harm out. Removing it would be like tearing down the parapets of a city during an enemy onslaught— being stripped naked of all defenses. Unthinkable.

And yet . . .

She snapped her notebook on all her arguments and walked into the closet that was large enough to double as a dressing room. When she reached to the back of the rack where the new gown hung under her coat, it wasn't the sound of swishing silk that filled her ears, however, but a familiar, hissed whisper, "Cover up. Cover up!"

Mother! I forgot about you. I'm getting things out of order, aren't I? Kyle said I had to deal with you first. She hung the caftan back in its concealment. Her long-sleeved, high-necked gown would do very well for tonight. A potato sack would do, really. Tom would never notice. Maybe she should take a marking pen and put statistics all over her lingerie—the ultimate in dressing to please her man.

Laura came out of the closet and looked at the clock— almost midnight. That made it nearly two o'clock in Houston—hardly a propitious hour to initiate a long-distance mother–daughter reconciliation. Laura knew her sense of reprieve was cowardly—but she welcomed it anyway. Maybe she'd feel more like confronting her mother tomorrow. Unlikely, but she wouldn't feel any *less* like it than she did right now.

Then she turned to Tom. There was one more difficult subject she had to broach, and this one might as well be now. "Tom—"

"Hmm?" He looked up and rubbed his eyes.

"I told Glenda we'd go to church with her and Kyle Sunday. That's OK, isn't it?"

He shrugged. "Why not?" And he turned back to his calculations.

"Good, I just wanted to check. I know you'll like them. They're really a neat couple. And, uh—" Now for the hard part. "Kyle suggested . . . that is, I was wondering . . ." She swallowed, hard. "Er—would you be willing to see Kyle too? I mean, not just at church, but—"

Tom turned so abruptly he knocked several papers to the floor. "You mean professionally? You want me to go to this guy and talk about my nonexistent sex life? No thank you! I may have my problems, but they're my own. I can handle them. I don't need some guy with a fancy degree telling me what to do in bed."

He stormed across the room and yanked the door open. "I'm going to see if the coffee shop's open. You might as well go on to sleep. I'll be hours yet on that report."

Laura turned and walked slowly up the stairs to the bedroom. As she passed the dressing room door she wondered, would she ever get to wear that red caftan for Tom?

Chapter 12

The next morning Laura drank an extra cup of strong tea to sustain her for the ordeal ahead. Then she placed the phone call to her mother before she lost her nerve. She sat biting on her fingernails as the phone rang in her ear.

"Hello, Mama. This is Laura."

"Laura, honey! What a nice surprise. How are you?" She was shocked when she heard her mother's voice across the wire. It wasn't the harsh, condemning voice of her conscience that memory brought back to her. She heard simply the quiet, southern drawl of an old woman. Laura hadn't realized her mother was getting old. She always thought of her just as she had been all those years ago—straight and sure and vigorous.

They visited for a few minutes about Laura's trip and the warm weather in Texas. She hadn't talked to her mother in months, yet they could have spent the whole time discussing the weather and the flowers her mother arranged for the church altar. Laura took a deep breath. "Mama, I need to talk to you. Really talk. About something serious. I've been seeing a—er, a doctor here—"

"Laura, baby, are you sick?" Laura felt more than heard the fear in her mother's voice.

"No, Mama. It's not that kind of doctor. I'm not sick, but my marriage is—"

"Laura! You and that man aren't getting a—divorce?" The last word was almost whispered, as if someone might be listening at the door.

"I certainly hope not. I'm doing everything I can to prevent it. And his name is Tom, Mama. Now, please, don't interrupt. This is very hard for me to say—but Dr. Larsen said I had to talk to you about this because a lot of the problems are caused by the way I was raised—"

"I raised you to be a good, God-fearing girl, young lady, and there's nothing wrong with that! Are you seeing one of those secular humanists? I've been hearing preachers talk about them on television—"

"Mama! I said don't interrupt. Now you've got to know that because you taught me that sex was bad—even with my husband—Tom and I have never been as happy as we could have been—as we should be."

Across the miles Laura could see the thin lips tightening. "Laura, if you've called me to talk dirty, I won't have it. I always did what I thought was best for you. I tried so hard to protect you. Maybe I tried too hard. But if I did, it was because I love you—because I didn't want anything terrible to spoil your life like—" She stopped so abruptly that for a moment Laura thought they'd been cut off.

"Mama? Are you there? You didn't want anything terrible to spoil my life like what?"

"Like anything dirty or sordid. I didn't want anything like that to come near my daughter. Laura, I loved you so much. You were such a beautiful baby. And you were all I had. After everyone—" Again, the abrupt halt.

"Everyone what, Mama? There's something you're not telling me, and I need to know. Please, Mama, my whole marriage—my whole life may depend on this. If you love me as much as you say, you've got to help me."

Laura couldn't believe it when the next sounds she heard were sobs. Her mother had never cried. Laura didn't think she was capable of it. "I never wanted you to know, Laura. I

117

couldn't bear the thought of having you despise me and turn against me like everyone else . . ."

"Mama, please." Now Laura was sobbing too.

"Your father—he was just back from Vietnam, so young and handsome in his Navy uniform. We all—my friends and I—we wanted to show our fighting men a good time. You've got to understand how it was then, Laura. There was so much controversy. Marchers were spitting on men in uniform, calling them traitors; brave men who risked their lives for our country had to watch long-haired thugs burn the flag they had fought for. All those hippies demonstrating for free love and no war—what did they know? If men like Joe hadn't fought to keep those good-for-nothings—"

"Yes, Mama. I studied all about that in American history." Laura gave an impatient sigh.

"But you have to understand, Laura. I wasn't loose or wild. I was a good, patriotic American girl who cared about our country. I was never a bad girl. Never before . . ."

"Of course you weren't."

"But everyone said I was then. They said I was dirt. Joe moved to another base before we knew I was—er—before we knew you were coming. Of course he promised he'd be back, but—"

"Mama, are you saying you weren't married?"

Her only answer was a sob.

"Didn't you write to him or call him or anything?"

"I tried. He never answered. I don't know. Maybe he was sent back to the war and got killed. I don't know. But when my condition got obvious, my family said they'd be guilty of my sin if they condoned it by putting up with me."

"They kicked you out?"

"Well, not exactly. They sent me to a home. If I hadn't been taught that suicide was a sin, I'd probably have taken care of the whole thing right then. But after you were born and you were so beautiful, I couldn't help but be glad I had you in spite of everything. But I was determined to raise you so you'd never get into trouble like I did. I didn't want you to have to go through anything like that." The voice on the wire rang with triumph. "And I did it too. You were always a good girl, Laura."

Laura sighed. "Yes, Mama. I was always a good girl."

"Laura, you've got to understand. You were all I ever had. Laura . . ." Suddenly her mother sounded old and alone and afraid. "Laura, don't hate me. Please. I tried so hard . . ."

Help me. Laura knew this was the moment. She had to say it. *Make the words come.* But tears came instead of words— washing, cleansing, healing tears. And then, finally, "Mama, I love you. Thank you for trying to do the right thing. I understand now. I really do."

For several moments both women sat there and cried, the telephone carrying their heartache to each other.

"God bless you, Laura."

"Yes, Mama. And you too. And, Mama, you come visit us sometime. How about Christmas? We'll send you a ticket . . ."

When the call was concluded Laura sat, just staring at the phone, but her mind was seeing a picture of her mother that she could never have imagined: her mother, young and pretty, laughing and in love with a young sailor. *Oh, Mama— all those years. It didn't have to be that way between us. Maybe we can make up for a little of it now.*

There would still be problems—they were inevitable. They would need many, many more talks, but this first step was an enormous one.

Laura heard the alarm clock ring by Tom's side of the bed. He had worked most of the night. Now he'd be getting up to phone his report to Phil. Dear, hard-working Tom. Was Kyle right? Now that things were better between her and her mother, would they be better between her and her husband?

The bells of the city announced Sunday morning. The carillon tower down by the harbor chimed for the blue skies and white clouds overhead while the tower bells of Christ Church Cathedral rang to the glory of God's handiwork in the autumn trees and bright flower gardens around them.

"Let's walk to church, Tom. I think it's only about three blocks." Laura slipped the jacket of her hunter green suit on over an ivory linen blouse and picked up her briefcase, which she often used simply as a purse. Tom agreed to the idea of walking, and as they began the gentle uphill climb the bells quieted, leaving the stage to the gulls calling overhead in the clear air. Laura slipped her arm in Tom's and took a deep breath. "Hmm, the air's so fresh. It's as if the whole day has been washed clean."

Maybe this wonderful fresh air was an indication of a whole fresh approach to their marriage. Laura realized she had made a giant stride forward with her mother. Now Tom. She hadn't given up on her hope he would agree to see Kyle for counseling. If only their meeting today could be successful; if it could somehow pave a way to a better future.

Laura was right about the walk being only three blocks, but they were three very long blocks, largely uphill, so in spite of the pleasure of walking in crunchy leaves, she was glad when they turned the corner and faced the gray and beige stone cathedral. Laura stood for a moment, looking up in awe at the massive square towers. "It looks as if it could have stood in Europe since medieval times, doesn't it?" Then the bells in the tower began chiming right over her head, ending all dialogue.

Kyle and Glenda were waiting for them in front of the Gothic-arched door. This was the first time Laura had seen her new friends together, and she was struck with what a charming couple they made. Glenda's freckled freshness and Kyle's dark intensity were the perfect foil for each other. She thought of her own Gwendolyn and Kevin. Gwen's auburn pageboy was longer than Glenda's, while Kevin's dark hair was just like Kyle's, but his cool gray eyes were nothing like Kyle's snapping black ones.

Laura introduced Tom. She thought there was a certain wariness in the handshake he offered Dr. Larsen. She hoped her anxiety for the men to become friends wouldn't cause tension between them.

"I'm glad you're a few minutes early so we can show you around a bit. This is a very special place." Glenda led the way into the cool, high-vaulted nave with its pointed arches reaching heavenward like hands folded in prayer, then stopped at the baptistery and pointed to the stained-glass windows depicting children of all nations approaching Jesus. "See the white dove in the center window? The panes weren't in yet when the first baby was baptized here. Just as the service began, a white dove flew in, circled around, then perched on the ledge until the service was over."

"Oh, my goodness, that sounds like foreshadowing," Laura said. "I wonder if that child grew up to be a preacher or teacher or something special."

"Makes you wonder, doesn't it? Wish I knew." Glenda ushered them down the side aisle. "Look across at the windows: Those are the 12 apostles, but the lower part of each window shows an activity of modern life and work. I like the idea that that's holy too. But here, this is what I wanted you to see." She stopped beneath one of the great stone pillars supporting the arched ceiling and looked upward. "This is the robin pillar. An intrepid little robin built her nest up there, and construction at that point had to be stopped until her family was fledged, so they put a stone model of her and her nest atop the pillar to mark the spot."

"What a rich heritage to worship in." But Laura's comment was lost as all 3,000 of the organ's pipes signaled the beginning of the service. Only her thoughts continued. This was the first time for her and Tom to worship together in ages. Tom was always so busy. He had dropped his Scout troop long ago, and it seemed they lost touch with their church friends who were now wrapped up in raising young families.

Could this service help bring them together? Kyle had talked so much about the spiritual aspects of intimacy, about marriages dying spiritually. Could they find their way back to each other here in these beautiful surroundings?

They took seats near the front in the dark wooden pews. "The choir screen is from Westminster Abbey, and the bishop's chair still has scars from the London Blitz, and the pulpit is carved from a 500-year-old oak tree from England," Glenda whispered just before the white-robed dean and assistant priests entered down the center aisle. Laura's attention shifted to hymnal and prayer book.

Glenda noticed Laura's fumblings with the prayer book and handed her one open to the correct page just in time to read the collect with the congregation, "Almighty God, unto whom all hearts are open, all desires known, and from whom no secrets are hid; cleanse the thoughts of our hearts by the inspiration of thy Holy Spirit, that we may perfectly love thee, and worthily magnify thy holy name; through Christ our Lord. Amen."

Laura hoped her lack of familiarity with the liturgy wasn't too apparent to those around her, but her heart thrilled with the service. She had always wanted to worship in one of the great cathedrals of the world. She loved the feeling of tradition and continuity—the sense of connectedness, knowing that Christians around the world had been worshiping with these prayers and forms for hundreds of years. She looked sideways at Tom. Were his thoughts perhaps akin to hers? Was he, too, realizing how much they had missed in leaving worship out of their lives? His immobile features gave no clue.

The dean ascended the stairs of the pulpit carved from that 500-year-old oak, and in spite of all the ancient traditions, the message was absolutely new and fresh to Laura's ears. "Be generous to one another, tender-hearted, forgiving one another as God in Christ forgave you . . ." The very scripture Kyle used in telling her she needed to forgive her mother. At first a warm glow over the phone call filled Laura's heart. She had done the right thing. It hadn't been easy, but she had persevered against the difficulty and she'd done it. She had forgiven her mother.

Then the glow was replaced with a stab as she looked at Tom sitting in stiff profile beside her. Well, yes, she had forgiven her mother. And that was all Kyle had said she had to do. But her conscience wasn't so easily put off. What about Tom? What about her husband and that—that other woman? Had she forgiven him? Could she forgive him?

Good grief! She suddenly felt defensive. *What is this? I'm getting it from every direction. Can't I have a break? What about Tom? Why can't he do something for this relationship? After all, I'm the wronged one here.*

". . . We will never be commanded to do what we will not be enabled to do. But you must first *want* to forgive . . ." Her answer came from the pulpit as clearly as if the priest were reading her thoughts. And he used almost the same words

Kyle had used, ". . . and once you have forgiven, you must be willing to trust the person who wronged you . . ."

Trust him? Wait a minute. I believe Tom when he says nothing really happened. But how can I keep from thinking, "What about next time?"

". . . Now, being willing to trust and trusting aren't the same thing. A little common sense can be useful here. I would like to suggest two guidelines you can apply. First, ask yourself, have you known this person to be honest in other areas? In business, in social obligations, can their word be trusted?"

Oh, yes. Tom's absolute reliability is one of the things I've always loved most about him. If he says he'll be there, he will be— and not even late.

". . . And then, ask yourself, has this person repented? If they have asked God's forgiveness and your forgiveness, then you must forgive and forget as freely as God has promised to do . . ."

Well, he apologized for hurting me—I don't think that's quite the same thing. Of course, if all he really ever did was hug her, I don't suppose that would require too much of the sackcloth and ashes thing. The trouble is, I don't really know what Tom feels about anything anymore. I didn't realize we had grown so far apart.

". . . and remember, if you forgive others the wrongs they have done, you will be forgiven; but if you do not forgive others, then the wrongs you have done will not be forgiven."

All through the offertory hymn and the continued congregational readings and responses, and then, even while kneeling at the Communion rail beside Tom, Laura kept thinking, *Forgive. Forgive and trust. Forgive and trust and forget. I can say it. But can I do it?*

All stood for the final prayer: "Almighty God, whose kingdom is everlasting and power infinite, have mercy upon us all, through Jesus Christ our Lord, who with Thee and the

Holy Ghost liveth and reigneth, ever one God, world without end. Amen."

Laura walked stiffly down the aisle. Now the stones around her seemed so cold and forbidding. She had come with such high hopes: for her and Tom to find a special bonding through worshiping together, for Tom and Kyle to begin a friendship, for her to find the ability to forgive. Well, that hadn't been one of her goals, but it was amazing how on-point the sermon was.

And perhaps she had moved closer to forgiving Tom. But she had felt no intimacy in their shared worship. They had knelt together, prayed together, even taken Communion side by side, but there must be something more.

The autumn brightness made her blink as they emerged onto the church steps. "Kyle and I are going to the Captain's Palace for dinner—come with us," Glenda invited.

Laura was delighted. There had been no opportunity during the service for Tom and Kyle to become really acquainted. Glenda's invitation was perfect. Now the men could get to know each other, Tom could get comfortable talking to Kyle. After all, there was nothing like food to bring people together.

And nothing could have made a more perfect setting for their Sunday meal than the historic Victorian mansion on the point overlooking the blue and silver harbor. The long white *Princess Margurite* liner with her distinctive union jack smokestacks stood serenely at anchor while on around the bay the Empress reigned over her domain.

"The Captain's Palace claims to be the smallest hotel in the world," Kyle said as Laura turned her attention from the window and looked up at the twinkling crystal chandeliers hanging from a frescoed ceiling.

"How small?"

"They rent one room."

Laura laughed, but Tom didn't react.

"But don't worry," Glenda said. "Their quiche lorraine is terrific."

"The fresh Sooke oysters are my favorite," Kyle said.

"I think I'll stick with chicken." Tom snapped his menu shut. Laura was sure—almost—that he didn't mean his comment to sound so dismissive. Perhaps if they left the men alone . . . "Would you show me the way to the ladies' room, Glenda?"

Glenda jumped up and led the way.

Laura grabbed her arm as soon as the door closed. "Well, tell me. Did you make an appointment with Kyle?"

"No. Yes. Well, in a way. I guess my acting skills aren't as good as I thought. He saw through it."

"Oh, too bad. You should have had a friend call for you."

"Yeah, probably. But I don't know—just the fact that I was desperate enough to try the ruse seems to have gotten his attention. He promised we'd have a serious talk."

"Great. When?"

Glenda shrugged, smiling weakly. "Soon."

"Mmm, well, hold him to it."

They returned to the table to find the men sitting in silence.

"Tom, why don't you tell Kyle about your work. I tried to explain it to him, but the machinations of higher economics are beyond me." She hoped she sounded bright and encouraging rather than desperate and pushing.

"My company develops low-rate investment instruments to put investors and real estate developers together. Inflation protection is my specialty."

"That sounds interesting. What kind of property do you do?"

"Residential."

Silence followed Tom's abrupt reply. "Captain Pendray, whose home this was, came here seeking gold," Glenda jumped into the breach. "But he found his fortune in making soap for the other prospectors. He put in some special antiseptics that helped control lice."

Laura shuddered, then forced a little laugh. She noticed a guest observing them with a smile from a nearby table. *I suppose we do make a good-looking party. Attractive couples, apparently well-suited to each other—none of our troubles showing. If only we were both living the serene lives we portray.*

Then she took a really close look at Kyle. He looked truly haggard behind his surface smile and stylish glasses. Just knowing Glenda's desire to be able to soothe and share his troubles made her want to reach out to them both.

And Tom. She turned sideways to study the clean, handsome lines of the face she loved. The bright sun coming in the bay window mercilessly revealed tiny tension lines around his eyes and mouth. Were these all the result of their marital problems? Or was there something else? Something she didn't know?

And how could she deal with what she didn't know? Her one hope of getting Tom to open up was her now obviously failed attempt to get him to talk to Kyle. Another failure to chalk up.

But maybe the day hadn't been a total loss. She had hoped to see a change in Tom; instead she had discovered a change in herself. Well, at least she had encountered a new question. Maybe even considering the need to forgive Tom was progress. And she could hope that changing herself would change Tom. She had to have something to cling to.

Chapter 13

They spent the evening reading. In the same room, but miles apart. Laura's eyes were on her book, but her mind was elsewhere. *It wasn't like this at first. We used to spend hours curled together on one end of the sofa. Even when we sat in separate chairs with our own books there was still a connectedness, an emotional closeness, as if we were inside the same bubble.*

Tom rattled the *Wall Street Journal* as he turned a page. Laura looked up and the date on the paper caught her eye. "Oh, Tom, your mother's birthday is next week. Why don't you take that plate you bought for her back to the gift shop and ask them to mail it so she'll get it on the right day?"

Tom glanced at Laura over the top of his newspaper but didn't reply.

She tried again. "Sorry, were you lost in your reading? I said—"

"I heard you. I didn't buy any plate for my mother."

"Yes you did. I was there. A delicate country springtime scene with a gold edging—"

"I remember the plate. It's not for my mother." He folded his paper with deliberation and placed it on the coffee table.

"But you said—"

"No, *you* said. And I chose not to argue with you."

A sudden fear made Laura's throat constrict. "Tom, who did you buy that plate for?"

"Now don't get upset, Laura. You didn't object to my

buying a piece of scrimshaw for Phil. So why should you object about—"

She knew. "About your buying the plate for Marla?" Her tones dropped an ice cube with each word.

"Look, it's business. I've tried and tried to tell you that."

"Business. Right. Except Phil is your partner and Marla is one of maybe 20 real estate agents you deal with. I'd ask what makes her special—only I don't want to be told. It isn't that I don't know the answer. I just don't want to hear it."

She got up and moved toward the door.

Tom sprang to his feet and gripped her arm. "Laura, listen to me! You don't understand at all. Marla isn't just a real estate agent. I need her."

Laura wrenched away with a sob, her hands over her ears. "I said I didn't want to hear it!"

He took her arm again and turned her to face him. "Well, you're going to hear it anyway. I need Marla, but not in any sordid way you obviously have in mind. Marla is the investor backing this Kansas City project. Her family is wealthy—very, very wealthy—and she believes in the future of this investment."

Laura blinked. "The project that's supposed to put Marsden and James on a solid footing financially?"

"That's the one. Clear over the top. Next stop, the big board on Wall Street."

"But couldn't you get financing somewhere else?"

"Probably—given considerable luck and plenty of time—two things we don't have. If this deal blows, we don't have a plan B. We'd have to start from scratch looking for a new one."

"But there must be others."

"Not of this size. We have some smaller things going, but even with the smaller ones, finding them and packaging them takes time and effort and nervous strain. Fine for me; I thrive on it—"

"But Phil . . ."

"That's right. If we can reach his goal, he'll retire and he and Lois should have lots of good years left. If not . . ."

Laura sank down on the sofa. What was he saying? That he had made love to Marla for her money? No. No matter how much it sounded like that, she could never believe anything so despicable of Tom.

But what about these other issues? What could she say? Everything inside her wanted to yell and argue that their marriage was more important than any business deal. She'd gladly go back to their presuccess days for the sake of having everything right—really right with Tom. But she couldn't be so selfish. Phil and Lois had stood by them through all the lean years. And Lois had been like an aunt to Laura. Lois was the only person with whom Laura had shared her agony over her childlessness. She couldn't choose her own happiness over theirs.

Things were coming at her too fast, much faster than she could handle. She had just begun to clear her own image of herself, gain some understanding of who she was and why, when she found she had to confront her mother. She was only a few hours clear of that barrier when she discovered she must also forgive and trust Tom. And now—accept Marla? Forgive Marla? No way.

She couldn't even think about that. One thing at a time. There was too much to work through with Tom yet. "Tom, I'm not through this yet. Actually I'm sinking deeper. Won't you help me? Won't you see Kyle with me, please?"

Tom looked thunderous.

Her voice was barely above a whisper. "Not for your sake. For mine. I need help."

★ ★ ★ ★ ★

Tom and Laura sat in the brown leather wingback chairs with Kyle across from them in a smaller chair he pulled around from his desk. Kyle looked so drawn and worried that Laura couldn't help wondering if they should trade places, but Dr. Larsen was, as always, keeping the session on sound professional lines. ". . . that, of course, is the core of the problem—growing apart rather than together." He waggled the eraser end of his pencil at them.

"And intimacy—physical and spiritual—which is the core and essence of marriage—can only be achieved by working together. Couples too often let their problems get between them. Then when they swing at the problem they miss and hit each other. You have to stand side-by-side and face the problem together."

Laura was quiet for a moment. She so wanted Tom to say something. To give some indication of his feelings. But he didn't. So she went ahead. "I think I see what you're saying. You're really talking about a whole lifestyle of love. That's as much about working together as it is about loving each other." She crossed her hands over her chest. "It's like a—a vocation. Does that sound sacrilegious?"

Kyle smiled. "Not at all. A Catholic friend of mine says that loving intimacy in marriage can be—should be—a means of grace. He likens it to prayer in the life of a celibate. The great mystics—Pierre Teilhard, St. Theresa, Julian of Norwich—experienced a passionate, ecstatic intimacy with God in the higher states of prayer. It's an exultation a husband and wife can achieve together in marital love."

Laura felt overwhelmed, embarrassed at the thought of such complete abandonment and yet desired the experience even as she shrank from it. *I am come into my garden, my sister, my spouse: I have gathered my myrrh with my spice; I have eaten my honeycomb with my honey; I have drunk my wine with my milk: eat, O friends; drink, yea, drink abundantly, O beloved.*

"It's the whole concept of a sacrament—a visible playing out of the Divine/human relationship. We need to experience the roles of lover and beloved in human terms in order to be able to understand being loved by the Divine. The Bible is full of such imagery: God and creation, Jehovah and Israel, Christ and the Church . . ."

I rose up to open to my beloved; and my hands dropped with myrrh, and my fingers with sweet smelling myrrh, upon the handles of the lock. I opened to my beloved; but my beloved had withdrawn himself, and was gone; my soul failed when he spake: I sought him, but I could not find him; I called him, but he gave me no answer.

"In marriage man and woman are given the gift to love each other as God does, with God's love working through them. First to each other, then to reach out to others around them—loving their children, church, neighbors. The husband and wife are transformed into living symbols of the God who is love."

It all sounded so wonderful. And so far beyond her grasp. *O my dove, that art in the clefts of the rock, in the secret places of the stairs, let me see thy countenance, let me hear thy voice; for sweet is thy voice, and thy countenance is comely. Take us the foxes, the little foxes, that spoil the vines: for our vines have tender grapes.*

Laura looked at Tom. What was he thinking? Were Kyle's words reaching him? Was his silence rejection of the whole idea of love being spiritual as well as physical? If only she could know. Tom's head was turned just slightly to reveal the line of his hair neatly clipped at the base of his head and the neckline above his collar. She longed to run her fingertips over that smooth skin. Then his hand moved on the arm of his chair and the broad gold band on his finger caught her eye. She put that there. That was her ring—her pledge—the symbol of her life with him.

"True marital oneness is a foretaste of heaven. It's a glimpse of the glory of God. Sacramental intimacy, far from being shameful or selfish, is a means of bringing God's grace into our lives."

My beloved is mine, and I am his: he feedeth among the lilies. Until the day break, and the shadows flee away, turn, my beloved, and be thou like a roe or a young hart upon the mountains.

"The tender concern and self-abandonment of sacred intimacy must be the mark of your daily life—not just half an hour before bedtime, but in all those largely trivial encounters that gradually weave the web of your closeness. We're talking about an atmosphere in your home, a total awareness of each other. Sex shouldn't be an isolated event, but something a husband and wife do together in the same loving context that they do everything."

The image Kyle's words were creating in Laura's mind was almost too wonderful to be contained—a home filled with quiet joy. "That's absolutely beautiful. Doesn't it sound unbelievably wonderful, Tom?" She rushed on to cover his silence. "But I don't think I could ever achieve anything like that."

"You can't. Not on your own."

No, but it seemed to be all up to her. Had Tom caught even a glimpse of the vision? "What do I—we—have to do?"

"Well, first of all, hearing this once is a nice start, but it can take years to internalize these concepts into natural behavior. You'll need to continue with the psychological understandings and the healing you've begun. And always work for complete sharing and openness between the two of you in all areas of your life. Learn to think of the welfare and happiness of the other person first—never seeking *my* will, or even *our* will, but looking for what's *right*.

"It's not going to happen overnight, or only during love-making. I'm talking about the constant state in which you live together."

Tom sat so quietly he could be asleep. His eyes were shadowed, giving no clue to his thoughts. *Come, my beloved. Let us go into the garden* . . . "Laura," Kyle's voice made her jump. "A while ago you used the term 'vocation'—a spiritual call. That's exactly what marriage is—a spiritual call from your Creator to the joyful intimacy He created you for."

Laura looked at Tom. *Arise, my love, my fair one and come away.* Her glance dropped shyly when he turned her direction. The idea was wonderful. But putting it all into action . . .

"Did an aura of desire exist between you when you were engaged?" Oh, dear. Now Kyle was getting directly personal. What if Tom walked out? Still, the question brought warm memories flooding back. She couldn't help nodding.

Kyle answered her with a nod. "And that glow can be maintained. Better yet, it can grow throughout your married life. If you work together."

Laura sat close to Tom on the drive back to the hotel. The reincarnation of that aura of desire they had once shared grew inside her. Surely it would spread to Tom. Surround and engulf him. With this they could build a shining wall of love around them that even Marla and her pots of gold couldn't scale.

Laura snuggled closer. Miraculously, Tom put his arm around her. She felt the warmth of his touch spread all through her. And for the first time in years it didn't end in a cold chill with the thought that this would lead to something else—something dirty. She could stay there, warm and comforted in the circle of her husband's arm, savoring the rightness of it, secure that this was her place. "Tom?"

"Hmm?"

"What did you think—about what Kyle said?"

"Sounded good. All theory, of course."

"But if we could achieve something like he talked about?"

"It'd be great."

Laura let out a deep sigh. She hadn't realized she had been metaphorically holding her breath for so long. It was all right then. Tom agreed. They would work together to build a marriage of shining radiance. "Oh, Tom, thank you! I so hoped you'd feel like that."

"Of course. Everybody wants a good marriage."

Back in the room he put his papers down. "Let's get some dinner."

"Yes!" Laura, who had just perched on the sofa, jumped up. "Let's celebrate! And I know just the place." She scrambled for her map. The Old England Inn would be the setting for their celebration—the setting for the beginning of their real honeymoon. The honeymoon they should have had seven years ago.

A short time later they entered the world of the Elizabethan coaching inn, and Laura felt that this moment had been worth waiting seven years for. She stopped just inside the door. "Oh, Tom, wait. Let me just absorb this."

"It's the time machine you've always longed for, isn't it?"

"That's exactly what it is." Amazing. Tom understood. He was entering her world with her. Laura was almost afraid to talk for fear the vision would vanish and she'd be back in a world of fast food and computers. But even after she blinked several times, the vision remained substantial: the great hall all of heavily carved black oak; a high, copper-hooded fireplace with a roaring fire, guarded by a suit of armor; a wide, red-carpeted stairway leading to a lead-glassed dormer large enough to hold several 16th-century chairs and sofas; and before them a massive refectory table surrounded by tall Jacobean chairs.

And the whole scene cast in the glow of candlelight. "Just look at those candelabra." Laura pointed to the massive, branched candlesticks on the table.

The hostess in laced vest and mobcap had been standing back, but at Laura's remark she moved forward. "A little boy bounded through here one day and said, 'Oh, look! Plastic.' I wanted to hit him over the head with one—they're that heavy."

Laura laughed. "That would have been a weighty lesson, all right." She ran her hand over the table glowing with a patina raised by centuries of such touches. "Your antiques are marvelous."

"Yes, this table was owned by the Brontë family."

Laura withdrew her hand, fearful of desecrating so valuable an object, but the hostess smiled. "Everything we have here is absolutely authentic. The only reproductions are two chairs in the dining room, and they are 200 years old—reproductions of chairs that were 200 years old then."

Laura and Tom entered the dining room laughing over the concept that anything 200 years old could be considered a reproduction. They were seated in a corner table by a window where English ivy looked in on them and the lamppost on the village green revealed stone lions crouching atop ivy-covered pillars marking the way to the Tudor village street beyond. And over and around it all, permeating every corner and pore, were the opulent tones of golden, baroque music. Laura relaxed in her high-backed chair, letting the sound flow through her. "Mmm, that music's so rich you don't need food."

"You can get fat listening here—just like breathing chocolate at Roger's."

"That's it—this sounds like Roger's smells." Intimacy, Laura thought. An accumulation of tiny, shared delights.

They were waited on by liveried footmen in black velvet knee breeches with white silk stockings and gold-trimmed red jerkins over white shirts. With a flourish worthy of his uniform, their waiter presented platters of pink-centered English roast beef and crisp, golden Yorkshire pudding surrounded by a colorful variety of vegetables.

Tom savored a bite. "Mmm, roast beef as a high art."

"And what's more, not one of the vegetables is limp or soggy."

But far more wonderful than the food, the antiques, or even the music, was Tom. Her Tom, her husband, her beloved, sitting in the glow of candlelight across from her. Laura felt she could touch the special aura around their table. She was intensely alert to Tom, totally absorbed in him. And she felt this special rapport being returned to her as they held the center of each other's attention.

Had they at last found the key? Could it go on and on this way as Kyle said? It must. Now that she had glimpsed Paradise, nothing less would do. Laura knew she could never go back to the old mundane routine without this touch of magic in her life, without the "two shall be one" experience of a true marriage. And, of course Tom agreed. Even if he didn't exactly say so. All would be well now.

After a time a liveried footman entered their charmed circle and served stemmed glasses of English trifle, prepared from the recipe Escoffier created when he served Queen Victoria in Windsor Castle. The trifle was accompanied by Murchie's Old England Inn tea in a round pot wearing a red velvet cozy. And again, the richly wrought 18th-century music swirled around them, adding its flavor to the dessert.

Laura took tiny bites, stretching every second to its fullest, caught up in her resplendent vision of the future—their future.

A white-capped waiter entered the far side of the dining room and began snuffing candles, putting the dining room to bed. Only one other guest remained in the room—a single man who sat with his back to them, stooping over his plate. What a pity to be alone in such a romantic place. But Tom and Laura were together, sitting in the glow of their single candle—Tom and Laura, Laura and Tom, and the two shall be one . . .

In the hovering gold shimmer of that relaxed, stepped-back-into-history atmosphere Laura was thinking what fun it would be to go upstairs to one of the antique furnished rooms she had read about when, as if he read her thoughts, a footman appeared bearing a salver with cameo mints on a lace doily atop the check. "We'd like to invite you to go upstairs and view our rooms. The unoccupied ones are open."

With the music accompanying them like a royal procession, Tom and Laura ascended the baronial staircase. The atmosphere remained unchanged since the days when the inn was a private home, and Laura felt that it could be their home—the lord and lady of the manor retiring for the night.

The first room they peeked in was the Victorian room: high brass bed with a delicate lace canopy, floral carpet, rose-patterned wallpaper, and an old brick fireplace. "This bed is too fluffy, said Baby Bear." Laura put her hand in Tom's and they strolled on down the hall.

The next room was titled Edward IV: an enormous room with gilt mirrors, baroque chandelier, and purple velvet hangings on the bed. "This bed is too grand, said Papa Bear." Tom grinned at her.

Laura glanced up at the glittery golden heart set in the

stucco of the archway as they went to the room at the end of the hall, the Elizabethan: richly carved furniture, tapestry hanging, a red velvet curtained bed that might well have provided slumber for Elizabeth I. "This bed is just right, said Mama Bear." Laura said it with a laugh, but she longed to snuggle under that fur and velvet quilt with Tom.

They descended the stairs with slow steps. It was late—only the solitary guest sat in the dormer, his head bent over a book. In her heart, Laura bid farewell to each item: the cozy 16th-century sitting room, the armored knight by the fireplace, the Brontë's refectory table . . . As they exited Tom paused to pick up a brochure about the replica of Anne Hathaway's cottage in the adjacent Tudor village. "This looks interesting. Shall we come back tomorrow?"

Laura agreed enthusiastically. But as they drove toward the Empress she was thinking, *That will be lovely tomorrow. But first—tonight.*

Chapter 14

Late into the night Laura sat over her journal, still unable to believe what had happened. Tom breathed heavily on the far side of the bed. Even asleep his back looked angry.

I understand that I must be totally, ecstatically abandoned to Tom—utterly and joyously give myself to him. And I wanted to. I thought I could. But how could I when I felt so rushed? So unprepared?

And Laura's mind played the scene again: Wanting to take time for a bath, to go to her lover in satin and lace and perfume; longing to be touched—kissed—caressed—to hear Tom's voice expressing his thoughts and feelings in truly revealing, honest words; needing to feel desired and cherished as a person, as his wife, not just a body to give him pleasure. And then it came, the stifling, choking feeling that she was drowning, that she couldn't get her breath. It had nothing to do with impressions that God or her mother were watching. But how could she respond as Tom demanded when she couldn't even get her breath?

And Tom was so terribly angry—so much angrier than she'd ever seen him before: "I thought we agreed with all that stuff Kyle said—intimacy. Sounds great, huh? But after all those come-hither looks and touches all evening, it's still the same old Laura. Same old frigid rejection."

Laura bit her lip. Hadn't he heard *anything* Kyle said? Had they been sitting in different rooms? Months, years of shared experiences, Kyle had said. Not just one romantic dinner and then everything would be fine.

"Tom, I'm not rejecting you! I want you so much my body aches! But I can't just turn it on. I need more time."

"Well, that's just fine. Take your time. Take all the time you need. How about another seven years?"

It was to have been the best night of her life. It was the worst. Far, far worse than before because she could see nothing more she could do. She had glimpsed a flower-filled paradise, but when she entered it the frost had been there, producing buds that would not open and turning the full-blown blossoms brown and ugly. Her paradise was a garden good only for rocks, weeds, and thorns.

I have caught a bright vision of the eternal, only to have it snatched away. It's so cruel. I can't have it. Yet I can't live without it.

O Lord, do not rebuke me. This is a load heavier than I can bear. I groan alone in my heart's longing. O Lord, all my lament lies open before You and my sighing is not secret to You. I call You to mind upon my bed and think on You in the watches of the night, remembering how you have been my help. Hear me, O God, hear my lament. My whole being cries out to You. My heart pines with longing. I turn to You for counsel. How can I sing the Lord's song with a heavy heart?

The next morning the tension in the air felt like a static-filled radio at high volume. One thing was certain. The trip to the Tudor village was off. Tom hadn't spoken a word, but he didn't need to. Besides, even if he wanted to go, there was no way Laura could imagine spending the day like happy-go-lucky sightseers. They were scheduled to return home tomorrow anyway. Home? Would anyplace ever be home again with things like this between her and Tom?

Laura shrugged and pulled herself out of bed. Might as well begin packing. Her heart sank as she thought of the tea cozy gifts, the fancy sweets, the red caftan—everything that she had purchased in such high expectations of all that would follow. How could it have come to nothing? Kyle and Glenda apparently hadn't had their promised talk yet, either. She hated to leave having accomplished nothing.

She was in the back of the deep closet yanking at her suitcase when the phone rang. She heard Tom answer it. A muffled conversation ensued. Probably Marla. Laura shook her head. Fine. Let him make any plans he wanted to. She didn't care. She just couldn't fight anymore. She reached for her ivory turtleneck, rolled it into a ball and stuffed it in the corner of her bag.

"Laura, I'm sorry." Tom stuck his head in the dressing room/closet. "Change of plans."

She shrugged her shoulders. Change of plans? You sure could call it that. Dismemberment of their marriage was certainly the last thing in the world she had planned on.

"We've got an extra passenger for the excursion today." Excursion?

"Don't look so blank. Tudor village, remember?"

"I remember. But I didn't realize we were still going."

"Might as well do something with our last day. Won't be coming back."

No. They wouldn't. "Er—extra passenger?"

"Yeah, funniest thing. That was Darren, Kyle's little brother. Seems he's doing a project on Shakespeare at school and needs to visit Anne Hathaway's cottage, so he asked if he could go with us."

She shrugged again. Strange, she didn't realize Tom had told Kyle where they were going today. Not that it mattered. Nothing mattered anymore.

The television news was on in the background. "Highs today near *12?*"

"Celsius. Remember?"

"No. Poetry sticks like glue—no room left for math, I guess. What does 12 Celsius mean?"

"It means you'll need a jacket."

Laura pulled her turtleneck from the suitcase and took her blazer off a hanger. Tailored professionalism on the outside should help bolster the inside. At least she could hope having Darren with them would reduce the awkwardness of being alone with Tom after last night.

When they picked the boy up, however, it seemed likely she had overestimated the value of Darren's presence. The small, dark-haired youth was so silent as he sat withdrawn into one corner of the backseat that it was hard to remember he was there.

The drive back to the scene of last night's happiness seemed long and desolate without the glow that had accompanied them then. Was there nothing she could do to recapture it? Was there anything anyone could do? Their time with Kyle yesterday had been their final appointment. He had given her a book to read on steps to recovery and told her—and Tom too—to find a counselor to help them in Boise, emphasizing that they had just started on the path.

Well, if they had started on a path, they sure got on the wrong one somewhere. Was there any way she could find her way before it was too late? Or was it already too late?

Desperate to break the stony silence between them, Laura dug in her briefcase for her guide notes about what they were to see. "When the owners of the inn decided to build a replica of Anne Hathaway's cottage, they went to Stratford-on-Avon and got permission to photograph everything and take all the measurements of the original building." This was hardly Tom's style of real estate development, but she could hope the topic would interest him.

"You mean they did it themselves? Didn't just hire the Hathaways' architect and say we want one like it? A whole subdivision of thatched cottages—might have potential."

Laura smiled, appreciative that Tom was making an effort. "Isn't the personal touch great. They did it because they loved it—like Jenny Butchart hanging over the sheer rock cliff on the quarry wall in a boatswain's chair shoving handfuls of ivy into every niche and nook." She turned to the backseat. "What a rich heritage you have here, Darren."

He shrugged. "It's all right, I suppose."

No wonder Kyle was showing the strain of single parenting. Darren's intense, dark eyes evidenced an intelligent mind, but the boy seemed uncomfortable with himself. Laura sensed that he wanted to be liked—but was afraid to be. Poor lad, his parents' sudden death must have rocked him badly.

She wondered about Kyle's concerns. Darren didn't seem like the type to take up with a rough crowd—but then, what did she know about teens today? If what she glimpsed on MTV when Tom indulged in an occasional spot of channel surfing was any indication, she wasn't sure she wanted to know about the youth culture.

But this young man wasn't youth culture in general. He was a human being with a great deal of potential. And her friends' happiness depended on his getting on the road to developing some of that potential. She would love to help in some way. If she could only find something to draw him out. "Tell us more about your project, Darren."

"Project?"

"Something about Shakespeare—needing to see Anne Hathaway's cottage?"

"Oh, yeah. Oh, just the usual thing. Boring."

"Don't you like Shakespeare?"

"He's OK."

Now she was landed with two silent males. It was a good thing her characters in her head talked to her.

They went first to the Tudor village Laura had merely glimpsed from the dining room window the night before. Walking along the uneven sidewalk of Chaucer Lane, peering in the little bow windows of the shops, Laura was once again transported to bygone days. "It's so realistic. I keep expecting a chambermaid to yell, 'Guardyloo!' and dump a slop basin out of an upstairs window."

"That might be overdoing the realism just a bit." Tom glanced at his gleaming shoes. He never left the room without buffing them.

The village buildings were all replicas of famous Tudor structures, collected around a village green complete with stocks and presided over by gnarled old oaks and stately Douglas firs. Everything looked as authentic as if it had been wafted to that spot by a magic wand—or as if the visitors had been conveyed back in time and space. Costumed Tudor young women hurried by on their actual chambermaid duties since the replica buildings housed guestrooms. In the distance the voices of children laughed and called, sounding just as children must have sounded in the 16th century.

Laura pulled out her notebook and started to make a note.

"I'll take that for you." Darren's sudden words startled her so she almost dropped her papers.

"What?"

"Your briefcase. I'll carry it for you—leave you with both hands free to write."

"How nice!" She was almost speechless that he should be so thoughtful. But then, it was easy to see that he had been raised well. She hated to discourage his courtesy, but she really needed her bag. "Thank you so much, but it isn't heavy, and I need stuff from it all the time."

Darren jerked a nod and withdrew into his shell. Laura regretted having rebuffed his offer. Maybe she should let him carry her things even if it was inconvenient for her.

Perhaps Tom noted her dilemma. At least he took over some of the responsibility of hosting Darren by pointing out the signs on each of the buildings. The Harvard House—home of the mother of the founder of Harvard University; the Garrick Inn—dedicated to the greatest English actor of his time known for having revived Shakespeare's plays in their original form; the tavern where John Oglethorpe met with other pilgrims to plan their perilous journey to the new world . . .

Darren was polite, if unresponsive. But it was a joy to Laura to watch Tom relate to the youth. Now she saw how good he must have been with his Boy Scouts. How good he would be with his own son. If only . . .

"And now to what we came for, huh, Darren?" She turned with a smile that was only slightly forced. "The home of Shakespeare's wife." She looked at his hands stuck in his jeans pockets. "Didn't you bring note paper?" She ripped a sheet from her pad. "Here. And I've got an extra pen some-place."

"Nah, that's OK."

"No notes? Don't you have to write a paper when you get back?"

Darren shrugged. "I've got a good memory."

Laura laughed. "So do I. But not that good." She wondered about Darren's teacher. If he was bored in school, it could be the school's fault. She didn't know anything about the Canadian educational system, but perhaps Kyle should consider putting the boy in a private school.

They went on down the pleasant country lane to the cottage. The recent rain and cool nights had dulled the usual joyous profusion of the English cottage garden, but tiny black and brown birds still flew from bush to bush chirping their chickadee cheer, and the garden still wafted a country fresh herbal scent. Asters and white and purple Michaelmas daisies bloomed valiantly, and on one bush—a single red rose.

Oh my love is like red, red rose that's newly sprung in June— well, one in October could have inspired Rabbie Burns as well.

> *Till all the seas gang dry, my dear,*
> *and the rocks melt with the sun;*
> *I will love thee still, my dear,*
> *While the sands of life shall run.*

She looked at Tom further ahead in the garden. They had experienced them all: dry seas, melted rocks, scratching thorns, and killing frosts—and yet she loved that man.

A little cobbled path took them to the cottage door where the leather latch string was hung out for visitors. Tom pulled the thong. ". . . the only full-sized replica in the world, it was opened in 1959 to commemorate the visit of Queen Elizabeth and Prince Philip to Victoria." The period-costumed guide was just beginning her lecture. Laura caught her breath when the girl turned and revealed glorious strawberry blond hair hanging to her waist. The exact color of Marla's. If Tom noticed, however, he was a better actor than Laura suspected.

They began in the parlor, its flagged floor warmed by the red-tongued fire in the stone fireplace filling one end of the room and by the rays of sun sparkling gently through tiny diamond panes in the leaded windows. The main feature of the room was the high, stiff, wooden courting settee on which Anne Hathaway and William Shakespeare sat on those long-ago spring evenings when he came calling. "He was 18 and she 26," the guide said. "And their descendants are still living in the Stratford area. The Hathaways were prosperous farmers. Eight rooms is a large cottage."

The guide lifted a heavy wooden box from its stand near the dining table. "The Bible box. The family Bible was always kept locked up because it was the family's most prized possession. They valued it for many reasons. For spiritual guidance, of course, plus it contained all the family records, and then, it cost the earth—as did all printed matter in those days. It remained in the parlor during the day, until the father read evening prayers after supper. Then it would be locked and carried to the master bedroom—always the job of the father as the spiritual head of the family.

"We'll move on to the buttery now." She ushered her guests before her.

"Mind your head!" The guide's cry was just in time to stop a tall, red-headed man with stooping shoulders from cracking his head. "Sorry. 'Mind your head' is the perennial cry of the guides. The Victoria city building code required that our ceilings be eight or nine inches higher than the original, but tall men still have a problem. The men were about five feet, four inches in the Hathaways' days, and the women about four feet nine."

They stopped at the buttery—on the north side of the house with special ventilation for a cool breeze to keep fresh the butter and cheese made there. "And note this cupboard bearing the carved blessing, 'He that fear God Shall want Nev . . .' " The guide ran her fingers over the raised words and the last two letters that continued to the far side of the chest in evidence that the illiterate carver had been given the text by the village priest and didn't know how to space his letters. "This was a marriage chest. All grooms carved them for their brides in the 16th century."

"Isn't this fascinating." Laura looked up from her notepad with a big smile at Darren. "Are you getting plenty of information for your project?"

He shrugged. "Sure."

"What aspect of Shakespeare's life are you focusing on? Maybe I could get you some extra information." Perhaps the lad needed more encouragement with his studies. She was sure Kyle did his best, but with his long hours at work and all . . . another indication that Glenda's help was needed.

"Oh, nothing special. Just stuff in general."

Definitely something wrong here. The group moved on upstairs to the solar, a special sun room for the ladies to sew that also doubled as a guest room—further evidence that the Hathaways were well-to-do for their class. Then on through the parents' bedroom into Anne's room with its extra-wide bed to accommodate a serving girl or two as well as Mistress Anne. It was covered by a canopy, "which served to catch the fallings—bugs, mice, sticks—from the bare thatch above. Cottage ceilings weren't stuccoed in until the 19th century."

The guide moved them on through the brothers' room, where Anne's brothers and the men working on the farm all slept together on the floor. Then the others went back down to the kitchen. But Laura returned to Anne's room. She looked out the small dormer window to the garden below with its stone bench and birdbath at the far end. Visitors milled around the garden. The man who had almost cracked his head on the timber looked up at her. Oh, that was the man who had been in the inn last night. And he was still alone. Poor man, no wonder he looked so unhappy. Her gaze lengthened on across the field to the replica of Shakespeare's birthplace, only slightly closer here than the original buildings were in Stratford. How many times had Anne stood at her window and thought of William? Or watched him coming to her across the field? Or was Will sitting on the other side thinking of Anne? And even as he thought of her were Katherine and Petruchio, Hermia and Lysander, or Romeo and Juliet taking shape in his mind?

And what of Laura's pair of lovers? Gwendolyn and Kevin were floundering. Their creator's mind had been too occupied lately to provide a stage for them to play out their dreams—just as in real life Glenda and Kyle were kept apart by the pressures of life. But she felt Gwen and Kevin's unhappiness; and she ached to bring about happiness for all of them, as for herself and Tom.

But the distances were so great—less than a quarter of a mile for William to walk to Anne; how far for Gwen/Glenda and Laura to reach Kevin/Kyle and Tom? Somehow their lives were entwined with each other, reflecting each other like the pictures that had fascinated her as a child of a girl holding a mirror that showed a girl holding a mirror that showed a girl . . .

"Laura!" Oh, no. Tom was calling her. She turned abruptly and hurried down the narrow wooden stairs. This was exactly the shutting-everyone-else-out daydreaming that Tom hated.

She hurried to him. "Oh, Tom, sorry. I was just thinking how wonderful it would be to stay here while writing a historical novel!"

"Yes, you must come back," the guide agreed. "Come for Christmas. We wear our fancy velvet dresses and sing old English carols, parade a boar's head, have Christmas crackers—everything."

"Wouldn't that be wonderful!" Laura spoke the words with a brave smile, but her mind added, *If we're still together by Christmas.* Always that dark cloud hung overhead.

"Well, that was interesting," Tom summarized the

morning as they drove back over the Esquimalt Bridge. "What's on your agenda for the afternoon?"

"I have a whole list of spots I need to visit, places I just haven't worked in yet." She didn't need to return the question. She knew he'd spend the afternoon working.

"Well, get them finished up. We leave tomorrow evening, you know."

How well she knew. But she didn't feel any of the relief about it that she heard in Tom's voice. She couldn't go back with nothing solved. The progress—and the regressions—only left it more impossible to return to life as it had been. The wounds had been reopened. Now if they weren't healed properly they would fester, leaving amputation as the only recourse. That was how she thought of it—that "D" word—so common today that it was reported as a statistic in the daily newspaper alongside notices of other forms of death. She refused to allow it in her vocabulary. It was unthinkable. And so was the idea of accompanying Tom back to Marla's world unthinkable.

And now there was an added problem. Having met Darren made her care about him so much more. Not just because he stood a hindrance to Glenda's happiness, but for himself. "Right. But let's get some lunch first." She might not know much about kids, but she knew teenage boys were always hungry. She looked over her shoulder. "What time do you have to be back at school?"

"No time. I don't have to go back today."

"Oh, really? No afternoon classes?"

He shrugged. "Yeah, but they're no big deal. I called in sick this morning."

"You what!"

"I can imitate Kyle's voice. I'm pretty good at it."

"You mean we've been helping you play hooky? I thought

this was an authorized activity—a Shakespeare project."

"Yeah, but it's no big deal."

Laura couldn't believe what she was hearing. "Well, let's get something to eat. I don't want to cope with this on an empty stomach. Then we're taking you to your brother, young man. I want to know what's going on here." She looked at his lowered eyes and sullen face. "You didn't have any English lit project, did you?"

They pulled up at a small restaurant on a tree-lined side street in a mostly residential neighborhood. In his best Scoutmaster mode, Tom ushered the youth to a seat inside. Laura dropped her things on the bench across from them. "Order fish and chips for me. I'll be right back." She turned to the ladies' room.

A few moments later she heard a crashing chair and shouting male voice. She rushed back to the dining room just in time to see Tom dash out the door in pursuit of a fleeing Darren.

Laura was halfway down the sidewalk after them when she saw that Darren was carrying her briefcase. He clutched the handles, the shoulder strap flapping beside him.

Tom was doing a valiant job of keeping up, but the teenage boy was fleeter of foot and showed no signs of tiring. Darren would likely have made his escape if the briefcase strap hadn't caught on a fence post.

He stopped and yanked. Hard.

Laura cringed at the sound of her favorite bag ripping, but stopped, gasping with relief when she saw that Tom had a firm grip on Darren's arm. Her heart still pounding in her ears after the mad dash, she stooped to retrieve her briefcase. As she picked it up, her papers fell out and she saw that the damage had been far more severe than she realized. "Oh, and this was practically new. Look, the lining's all torn away—"

She lifted the black and white checked fabric lining and gasped.

"Owgh! Why you—" Tom's sharp outcry jerked Laura's attention to him. "The hoodlum bit me."

Darren vaulted the fence and disappeared around the back of the house.

"Let him go. Good riddance." Tom cradled his bleeding fingers in his good hand.

"Tom, call the police."

"Kyle can do that. I don't want him back."

"No, not about Darren. Look." She held out her ripped bag. Tiny plastic bags of white powder padded the inside of her briefcase like batting in a quilt.

Chapter 15

"One pound of heroin." The young officer in the crisp blue-black uniform of the city police shook his head. "More than $70,000 Canadian."

Laura looked at Tom. "That's $50,000 American." He supplied the math for her.

"Right." The policeman had red hair and freckles. His badge said Sgt. Monaghan. "It's sold on the street by the paper—about one-twelfth of a gram—for," he paused, "about $25 American. A paper will provide an addict with one or two hits."

"All that in my briefcase." Laura shook her head. "I noticed it was heavy. But I thought it was just the extra books." She thought for a moment. "But I don't see how it got there. I mean, wouldn't it take ages to put all these little bags in so neatly?"

Sgt. Monaghan shook his head. "Matter of a few minutes, I should think. For someone experienced, that is. Slit the lining with a sharp knife, the bags have the fixative already on them, then this quick-fix sealant to reseal the cut."

"I just can't believe I carried this day and night for two weeks and didn't have any idea." Laura's mind whirled with questions. "How—?"

"Thank you, Sergeant, that will do." A middle-aged, balding man in a tweed suit and plaid tie entered the room and introduced himself as Detective Inspector Snow. It was clear that he had not come to inform, but to be informed.

"Now, Mrs. James, you say you have absolutely no idea how the drugs got into your briefcase?"

"Of course not! Would we call you if we were smugglers?"

D.I. Snow made no reply.

"Obviously someone put them there when I wasn't looking. But I can't imagine when that would have been possible. My briefcase is hardly ever out of my sight. I all but sleep with it."

Her statement drew an ironic look from Tom.

Laura struggled on. "But obviously someone wanted me to carry it back to the States. I've heard that Seattle has a growing problem—"

"So if they wanted to get it to the States, why did they try a snatch here?" D.I. Snow leaned toward her.

"What! Darren? Part of a drug ring? No. He's just a mixed-up kid. He ran away because he didn't want to be turned over to his brother with a truancy—" Laura protested. But even before the detective voiced the question, her mind was asking—so why did he take your briefcase? She had no answer. "Have you gotten a hold of Kyle—er, Dr. Larsen yet?"

"We have. The boy hasn't turned up. We're looking for him."

With Tom's help Laura answered all the investigator's questions as thoroughly as she could. But there was little she could say. She really didn't know anything. Drug traffic in Victoria seemed as incongruous as a viper in Wonderland. But then, there was that serpent in the first garden. *Now the serpent was more subtil than any beast of the field which the LORD God made. And he said unto the woman . . .*

". . . So will you be willing to cooperate with us, Mrs. James?"

Laura jumped. Oh, no. She had spaced off again. No

wonder Tom complained. "Er—sorry. Could you just go over that again?" Actually, now she realized she had got some of the officer's words. Something about D.I. Snow's belief that the drugs were for the Canadian market and thinking it likely that Darren had gone into hiding from whoever put him up to the failed attempt. Therefore they probably believed she was still carrying their stash. So if she would just be willing to walk around Victoria carrying a similar briefcase (they would need the original as evidence)—

"No way. You're not using my wife as a lure for your criminals. Where's the American consulate? We don't have to put up with this. My wife is an innocent bystander, and we're going home tomorrow. You have your drugs."

"Of course, Mr. James, you can call your consulate in Vancouver or your attorney or anyone you want to, but as drug traffic is such a major international problem and American-Canadian cross-border cooperation is so close, I expect you will be advised to assist us all you can."

Tom started to protest, but the detective continued. "Also, as the drugs were found in your wife's possession, I would strongly advise you to consider voluntarily changing your return reservations."

Tom's chair scraped against the floor as he jerked to his feet. "Are you threatening us with extradition? Or arrest? Now see here—"

"Tom." Laura put her hand on his arm. "I'm sure they can sort out their drug problem. But I'm worried about Darren. And what this will mean to Kyle and Glenda. Why would some ring of professionals enlist a mere schoolboy for a job like this?"

Young Sgt. Monaghan gave a winning grin. He seemed much more willing to answer Laura's questions than his superior. "Because they wouldn't want us to know drugs were involved at all. Some young delinquent snatching a bag for a lark wouldn't be a cause for a major investigation."

Laura flared. "Darren is not a delinquent! I want to know who put him up to this—and—" Something had been bothering her ever since Darren's phone call. "—How did they know where we were planning to go today so Darren could ask to go along?" She looked at Tom. "At first I thought you must have said something to Kyle. But, of course, you haven't talked to him since we made those plans."

Laura shivered. "Someone knows more about us than I like to think. Someone must be listening in on our conversations." Her face flamed red. Considering that they seemed to spend most of their time discussing—or fighting about—the most intimate details of their marriage, the idea of their room being bugged was unthinkable. But that wasn't the most important issue right now. "Don't you see, Tom—if Darren was put up to that amateur bit of purse snatching by some—some drug baron or something—he must be in real danger now." She turned to the detective. "I'll do anything I can to help."

"Laura—"

"Tom, we can't run out on our friends. I have to help."

Tom nodded. "I'll see about getting an open-end return." But he didn't look happy.

They agreed that tomorrow Laura should continue with the research schedule she had originally set for this afternoon. It seemed likely that whoever was supposed to receive the drugs knew Tom and Laura were about to leave Canada. That must have been what triggered the clumsy overt attempt. If they didn't know she had discovered the drugs, they would certainly try another snatch in the next 24 hours.

Laura glanced in her rearview mirror and gave a quick sigh of relief. Yes, the police were still right behind her. She had been at this for several hours now, and all was going fine. She hoped Tom's work was going as well. He had wanted to accompany her, but D.I. Snow insisted she go alone. Just as well, because later she had heard Tom making an appointment for this afternoon. Besides, she was safer now than if she had refused the set-up. Really she was. After all, how many visitors to the city got their own personal police escort? But then—how many needed it? She pulled in at a newsstand to buy one of the essentials for getting a feel for a city—a local newspaper. She stuffed her purchase in the look-alike briefcase, trying to make the action look natural before she walked on down the street to Marks & Spencer's.

Don't look over your shoulder. Don't look. You have to act natural. But no matter how many times Laura told herself that she couldn't get over the impulse to look. *Am I being followed? Will I recognize my stalker?* Now that she thought about it, she could see that someone had been there all along. So many little incidents that one never gave a thought to—the shadow behind the Queen Victoria statue, the face in the mirror at the castle, the hang-up phone calls—maybe they hadn't been Marla—the houseboy who got the wrong room . . . If only she could recall in detail what any of them looked like . . .

Focus on your research. You really do need to get this done. You do your job and let the police do theirs. That was another worry. More than wanting to look for her pursuer, Laura wanted to check to see that the police were there. She'd seen enough TV programs using the very scenario she was playing out in real life. And something always went wrong. The bad guys got to the cops first. The cops lost the person they were guarding . . . Laura gave herself a mental shake and sorted through her list. She had seen most of the essential service spots that might be important in setting a novel in a particular city: hospital, library, City Hall, department store, post office. Bank and pharmacy still to go. It would be so much more efficient just to hop in a cab and say, "Drive me." But that would insulate her. She had to stay vulnerable.

She gave a quick look to be sure her stakeout saw her, then got back in her car. Next on her list was a drive through a residential section of Victoria to see how the people really lived. As she drove toward the outskirts of town she was once again impressed with the variegated cultural background of the area: names like Duncan and Nanaimo stood on the same signpost. Still driving, she jotted a note on the pad resting on the seat beside her.

The areas she drove through were nice, quiet neighborhoods—middle-class homes with well-kept lawns, younger children riding tricycles on the sidewalks while their older siblings were at school. And as everywhere on the island, Laura was impressed with the greenness—no wonder the early English settlers felt so at home here.

As her wanderings took her farther from town the homes became newer, some individually built among their more established neighbors, others built in groups on the order of a subdivision. Because of Tom's work she was always interested in new home construction. She made a quick note to tell him about her observations here. She was always glad when she could talk to Tom about his interests.

A movement of traffic behind her caught her attention. She had been so absorbed in her work she had momentarily forgotten the ulterior motive to all this. But one look in her mirror told her she was still being followed. She was heaving a sigh of relief when the chilling thought struck her. That *was* the police in that little gray car, wasn't it? How could she be certain which lot was on her tail?

Suddenly the quiet of the peaceful neighborhood struck

her as ominous. She wanted people around her. Besides, she'd seen enough of the residential area. *Next corner, turn right and head back to town. But drive normally. Don't speed through this school zone.*

In the next street, though, something distracted her interest from the little car behind her. In spite of his jealousy over the attention she gave her fictional characters, Tom was truly first in her thoughts. And here was something Tom should see: a three or four block area with brick and wrought iron fence enclosing a partially finished housing development—just the sort of project Marsden and James liked to promote. Some homes appeared to be ready for occupancy, others had only the foundations poured. And everything a beehive of activity with workers, supervisors, and truckloads of equipment. But something was wrong.

She pulled over to the curb near one of the half-completed homes and watched, trying to figure out what was amiss. The supervisor in a dark gray business suit and yellow hard hat referred to notes on his clipboard as he gave orders to several workers loading two-by-fours onto a pickup. When one of the men climbed into the driver's seat and drove off, it clicked in Laura's mind. The whole scene was like watching a movie with the VCR running backward. They weren't constructing homes, they were deconstructing.

Now she looked more closely. Supervisors on a construction job shouldn't be wearing three-piece suits. These men looked like bank executives. The trucks weren't from lumberyards; the inscriptions on their sides said Saanich Storage. And across the street a signboard was being hammered into place by a grim-faced workman. Thinking of Tom's interest, she jotted down the pertinent information: Property offered by First Provincial Bank of Victoria, Wm. Eaton, Vice Pres., and the phone number.

Laura's stomach began telling her it was teatime. Amazing how quickly one's system could become acclimated to a new routine. What for the first few days was a charming novelty had now become a necessity. She could no longer get through the afternoon without a pick-me-up of scones and tea. She glanced at her guidebook. "The Cottage Tearoom, relaxed and cozy atmosphere away from the bustle of downtown business." That sounded just right. Besides, she noted, it was near Antique Row, which was another spot in that slightly off-the-beaten-track part of town that she hadn't visited yet. She shook her head; one could never really cover all the attractions Victoria offered.

There were no parking places along Fort Street, so she turned onto a quiet side street. Still no open spots. She slipped around a corner. Oh, there—people were parking on one side of the wide alleyway that divided the block. She turned onto the graveled passage and found a spot near a vacant lot. This was perfect, she could simply cross the empty lot and come out two doors from the tea shop. She tucked her books and precious notes under the seat, grabbed her brief-case, and stepped out.

" 'Ere now, that bag looks awful 'eavy. We'll just give you a bit of 'elp by carryin' it for ya."

Laura spun around. Her first reaction was to laugh. What were those men doing with tea cozies over their faces?

The laugh turned to a scream when she saw the length of metal pipe in the closest one's hand. She didn't mean to resist. Her stepping backward was sheer instinct.

The blow seared across the back of her head.

Chapter 16

Whither is thy beloved gone, O thou fairest among women? whither is thy beloved turned aside? that we may seek him with thee.

My beloved is gone down into his garden, to the beds of spices, to feed in the gardens, and to gather lilies. I am my beloved's, and my beloved is mine: he feedeth among the lilies.

"Laura? I'm here. Can you hear me?"

Tom's voice. Fuzzy and far off. Her beloved, calling her from his garden. "Yes, I'm coming. We'll gather the lilies together." But her voice was too weak to form the words. Besides, it was all dark in the garden. And it hurt to move.

Turn away thine eyes from me, for they have overcome me . . .

Sometime later she surfaced again. This time the room was quiet, only a soft light glowed in one corner of the room. The pain in her head was still excruciating, but at least she could think. She had gotten out of the car—three men in tea cozies. No, ski masks—the briefcase . . . They got the drugs! No, no, the police already had them. That was it, the police were supposed to have been there first. What happened?

Did they get there in time to get the men? Could she identify them? A voice maybe? One of them had spoken—a youngish voice, straining to sound tough.

"Oh, are you awake?"

No, that wasn't the voice. It was younger, a little British sounding.

"How are you, Laura?"

162

Tom! It was Tom. Laura opened her eyes. "Hi." She attempted a faint smile.

"Good, you're awake. Can you sip a little water? The nurse said—"

Laura started to shake her head, but it hurt too much. It was easier just to open her mouth obediently and accept the straw Tom was holding to her lips. The sip was all she could manage.

"Good girl. Now go back to sleep. I'll be here if you need anything." He brushed her forehead with his lips.

"I love you." Had she said that, or had Tom? Or had she dreamed it? *Thou that dwellest in the gardens, thy companions hearken to thy voice: cause me to hear it. Make haste, my beloved, and be thou like to a roe or to a young hart upon the mountains of spices.*

The next time she opened her eyes she felt really awake. The pain in her head had settled down to a dull ache that left room for other thoughts. Laura looked across the room to the big chair in the corner. Tom sat there. Asleep. The pale light fell across his face, highlighting his hair. Even in the dimness she could tell he was uncharacteristically rumpled.

The stab in her heart was far more severe than the pain in her head. She longed to reach out and caress his tousled blond hair.

She remembered now—she had been on her way to have tea. So this must be the next morning. *Did Tom sit with me all night?* She had heard his voice at some time as she drifted in and out of consciousness. "Tom, I love you." But her voice was too weak to penetrate his slumbers . . .

"Good morning, Mrs. James. Would you care for a bit of a wash? Breakfast will be coming in a few minutes."

This time the light was bright at the window. But the chair in the corner was empty. Laura looked at the white-capped nurse. "Yes, fine." Anything they wanted to do with her was all right. She just wanted to see Tom. Where was he? Had she dreamed him sitting in her room?

The warm cloth on her hands and face was marvelously reviving. "I'm just going to roll you up a bit now. The doctor said you could have some tea and a nice soft egg if you felt up to it."

There was nothing in the world Laura felt less up to than a "nice soft egg," but the tea and toast were welcomed by her empty stomach. She was just finishing her toast when the nurse returned with a plump little man she introduced as Dr. Jenkins.

He adjusted his dark-rimmed glasses and peered into Laura's eyes with a small light, then looked down her throat and felt cautiously over her head with gentle fingers. In spite of his care, though, the process made her wince.

"Well, young lady, how's the headache?"

"Still there, but better."

"We want to get some X rays of that lump on your skull to be sure there isn't a hairline crack under it. But do you feel up to talking to a visitor first?"

"Sure." Laura hoped he meant Tom, even if "visitor" was a strange way to refer to her husband.

"No more than 10 minutes," the doctor instructed.

Then the freckled face of Officer Monaghan appeared over her. Actually, she saw very little but the top of his red curls as his head was hung so low. "I'm so sorry, ma'am. The chief will apologize officially, but I had to come first. This shouldn't have happened. It was my fault." He produced a handful of brilliant bronze and yellow chrysanthemums from behind his back.

"Thank you." Laura tried to make her smile match the brightness of the flowers. "I'm not blaming you. I volunteered. But what happened?"

"We got stuck in the traffic when you made all those sharp turns."

Laura wanted to nod, but motion still hurt her head. "Yes, I was looking for a parking spot."

"We weren't far back. We caught two of them, but one got away. There were three, right?"

Laura thought for a moment. "Yes, three."

"And we recovered this." He held out the replacement briefcase that had earned this world-class headache for her. "The one ran off with this but stashed it in a bin a few blocks away. A street-cleaning crew found it." He placed it on the bed beside her. "When you feel like it, we'd be obliged if you'd go through it and tell us if anything is missing."

"Not likely. It was just maps and stuff. I keep my money and credit cards in my pockets."

"Right. Well, if you'd just take a look. Anything might give us a clue. I know you want this cleared up as much as we do. Do you think you could identify the ones we're holding?"

"They were wearing ski masks."

"Yes, I know, but maybe something about the way they stood, or their clothes?"

The nurse stuck her head in the door. "The doctor said—"

"Ten minutes, I know. I'll be right out, Miss Nightingale." He turned back to Laura. "Dr. Jenkins said you'll be released this afternoon if your tests are satisfactory. We'd appreciate it if you'd stop by the police station—just see if anything jogs a memory."

"You caught them in the act, isn't that enough?"

"You'd think so, wouldn't you? But they will probably claim they were just passing—that the one who got away was the mugger."

"I don't know what help I can be."

The nurse appeared in the doorway, but she didn't have to say anything. Sgt. Monaghan turned to go. Laura wanted to ask where Tom was, but the effort was too much. She slid off to sleep again.

She was being wheeled, bed and all, to the X-ray lab when she next wakened. The joy of waking was that each time she felt brighter and her head hurt less. But then the poking and prodding seemed endless as more extensive tests followed.

Finally they took her back to her room and the only sight she really cared about. Tom. "Laura, how are you?" He was freshly shaven, but his eyes looked haggard.

"Much better. Tom, thank you so much for staying the night with me."

"You knew?"

"Sort of. Off and on. But it helped a lot—knowing you were there." She reached for his hand.

"I couldn't have been anywhere else." He squeezed her hand until it hurt, then dropped it. "I was so worried . . . Laura, I've got a lot to tell you—" An aide came into the room with fresh ice water. "But not here."

Laura smiled. She wanted to hear what he had to tell her. But for the moment she was content just to lie there and look at the midday light on Tom's features as he stood by the window: his straight nose, his chiseled cheekbones, and the light in his eyes—that was what was different. In spite of the dark circles, his eyes had a kind of gentle glow that could warm a room. Or a heart. Gone was the stern look of the Edwardian disciplinarian that she so often encountered. Yes, she was anxious to hear what he had to tell her.

"Well, you're a lucky lady, Mrs. James." Dr. Jenkins bounced into the room holding a clipboard. You have a hard head, young woman. There shouldn't be any permanent harm from that encounter with a lead pipe. I'll prescribe some painkillers for the headache, and you can go when you feel like it."

"What about eating? Travel?" she asked.

"Eat all you can to get your strength up. You should be able to travel in a day or two—just be sure you're over any light-headedness before you fly. Any other activities are fine—just do whatever you feel like with common sense."

"I wasn't planning to go bungee jumping."

"I'm relieved to hear it."

A short time later the nurse wheeled Laura to the door of the Royal Jubilee Hospital, and Tom helped her into the car.

"Well, as the saying goes—you never know when you start out in the morning," Laura said as they pulled away from the curb.

Tom grinned. "That was yesterday morning. We'll try to keep things a little more routine today. But do you feel like stopping at the police station? They told me they needed to see you."

"Oh, yes. Officer Monaghan came up to see me before you got there this morning."

Tom pulled up before City Hall with its high arched windows and distinctive clock tower and helped Laura out of the car. "Are you sure you're up to this?"

"Might as well get the formalities over. I don't see what help I can be, but I have to try."

Laura supposed she would be asked to view a lineup—the sort of procedure one saw on countless television police shows. Instead, however, D.I. Snow received her formally with a very proper apology and ushered her into an interview room. A moment later Sgt. Monaghan brought in a tall, stooped man with red hair.

Laura bit her lip. Yes, maybe she had seen him before. Something about his posture, maybe? Or the ring in his left ear? No, she hadn't seen his face before. And yet . . . But something seemed wrong. Backward.

She scribbled a few words on a slip of paper and handed it to the sergeant. "Have him say this." She turned away so as to concentrate on his voice.

"That bag looks 'eavy, Lady. We'll just 'elp you with it."

Yes, the voice had the Cockney accent she remembered. But there was something else pulling at her memory. "It sounds the same, but—"

"Take him out. Bring the other one in," Snow ordered.

The man turned toward the door, and the window in the top acted like a mirror, catching his reflection. "Oh! It's him. The man in the mirror—at the castle. You were following me!"

"Prove it." The man shrugged and slouched out ahead of Monaghan.

It was the slope of the shoulders that made another memory click like a slide slipping into a projector. The man sitting with his back to them at the Old England Inn. That was how they knew where she'd be the next day. She shuddered, thinking of being watched so closely.

A moment later the door opened again. Laura gasped. She should have known—all those "fortuitous" meetings— "Monty!"

"Who?" Officers and suspect asked in unison.

Laura shook her head. "I don't know his name. I thought of him as Monty because we saw that exhibit of the Canadian Mounties—"

"You—I told you to leave my wife alone!" Tom lunged.

But Snow was quick with his restraining hold. "Franklin Tiegs, this is. Ironic you should call him Monty—the RCMP have had a lookout for him for some time, but never could get any proof."

"You still don't have any."

"You followed my wife all over Victoria like a lap dog!"

"That's not a crime."

"You put those drugs in her briefcase. How did you manage it?"

The accused clenched his square jaw.

"I think I know." Laura spoke up. "I was too airsick to work on the flight. I put my case in the overhead bin behind me."

"You knew customs might be watching you, didn't you, Tiegs?" Snow approached the broad, dark-haired man. "So you picked on a lady so innocent-looking they'd barely glance at her passport."

"I want to call my lawyer."

"I think that's an excellent idea." The officer started to usher his prisoner out.

"Wait." Laura stopped them. "What about Darren?"

"Darren?"

"Darren Larsen. The boy you put up to snatching my case yesterday."

Tiegs shrugged. "Never heard of him. I'll ask my lawyer if he knows him."

Back in their hotel room Laura rested in bed with a tea tray on her knees before Tom pulled up a small chair and sat beside her. "Laura, I apologize. About that Tiegs fellow."

"What do you mean?"

"The way I all but accused you of leading him on. Well, he is good-looking—"

Laura laughed. "In an awfully rugged way. Not my type."

"Yes, but if I hadn't been so blinded by my distrust, I might have been able to put it together far sooner that you were in danger. As it was, every time you jumped at a shadow I thought you were trying to keep something from me."

She nodded. "I know. And those hang-up phone calls—I thought they were Marla."

"Laura—there's so much I need—"

"Oh! Tom, I forgot. I promised I'd look through that bag. Hand it to me, please." He reached over and set the case beside her. "Thanks. Even the police must realize this is silly, or they'd have had me do it at the station. Still, I promised."

She dumped the contents on the green, flowered coverlet and began sifting through them: map, guidebook, newspaper, various pamphlets, notepad. No, just as she expected—all there. She tossed the notepad on the top of the pile and turned back to her tea.

"What's this? This isn't your writing." Tom picked up the pad and examined the scrawl on the cardboard backing. The square-looking letters were printed boldly, written in haste, but pressed deep into the cardboard: SANCTUARY.

Laura frowned as she squinted at the block letters. Definitely not her writing. And a nearly new pad. Who had been making notes on her paper? And why? Then she noticed the much lighter scrawl beneath. "Tom, what does this say? Can you turn that light up?"

Tom took the notebook to the window and held it up to natural light. "I can't read all of it, but that's definitely a D. I'd think Darren had autographed your notes, but he didn't have hold of the case long enough to write anything."

"No. Besides, I just started that pad. The one I used at Anne Hathaway's House is—" She gasped. "Wait a minute. Maybe he *did* have it long enough." She looked at the scrawl, added almost as an afterthought following the carefully incised letters above it. It was as if Sanctuary was the message, but then the writer suddenly realized the word might be meaningless without his identity. "Could Darren have been the third man?"

"Wouldn't you have recognized him?"

"I had less than a second. But suppose whoever put him up to taking my bag in the first place—"

"Not whoever. Tiegs."

"Right. Has to be. Well, suppose whatever hold Tiegs has over Darren, he forced him into a second attempt. This time Darren didn't drop the bag accidentally—he stashed it where he could hope it would be found—"

"And then ran off into hiding himself."

"Right. Hiding from everybody—Tiegs, the police, Kyle—"

"Not from everybody, or he wouldn't have bothered leaving a clue to his whereabouts."

Laura nodded. "Kyle must be out of his mind with worry. Call him, Tom."

"Do you think he'll know what this means?"

"If we're right about all this, Darren must have figured someone would understand it." She slumped back against the pillows. Tom would take care of everything. She could just close her eyes and . . .

"Laura, I'm so sorry! I wanted to come up to the hospital, but they said you couldn't have visitors." Glenda bent over the bed and hugged her. "How are you?"

Laura thought for a moment, then smiled. "Fine. Starving. My headache's gone."

Kyle examined the note Tom showed him. "Yes, that's Darren's writing. What does he think he's up to? How could he possibly be involved with a drug pusher? And to steal from you—twice! Believe me, when I get my hands on him—"

"No, Kyle." Laura held out her hand. "He's in some kind of trouble. He needs help."

"He'll need help all right when I find him. Can you make any sense of this?" He handed the pad to Glenda.

"Kyle, I know how worried you are about Darren," Laura began, "but try thinking of him as one of your patients, not—"

"Oh!" Glenda stood pointing to the word on the notebook. "I know where he is."

"You do?" Kyle looked amazed behind his silver-rimmed glasses.

"Yes. He's taken sanctuary in the church. You know—the medieval concept that a person was safe in a church if they claimed sanctuary."

Kyle scowled. "How do you know that? How would Darren know about such a thing?"

"I took him to see *The Hunchback of Notre Dame* one night when you had to work late. He loved it. He talked a lot about the concept of sanctuary afterward—the idea of being really safe and accepted someplace."

Kyle looked thunderstruck.

"He wants you to go to him." Laura said it softly; this whole thing was obviously an enormous blow to Kyle. "He wouldn't have left you the note if he didn't want to be found."

Kyle shook his head. "He left you the note."

"Me?" Now it was Laura's turn to be thunderstruck.

"He trusts you, not me."

"My notebook was handy, that's all."

"No, it's more than that. He's hiding, asking for you. He could have come to me. He could have run home. I'd have given him sanctuary there. But he was afraid of me."

"Would you have given him sanctuary? Or would you have lectured him?" Glenda asked.

Kyle shook his head. "I don't know. I tried so hard to do it right. I know what all the books say. I can help my patients. But I fail with my own brother."

"Maybe because you were trying too hard. Trying to do it all yourself," Glenda suggested.

Kyle nodded. "The great, self-sufficient, all-knowing Dr. Larsen—Physician, heal thyself."

"We should call the police," Tom said.

"That would rather violate the whole sanctuary thing." Laura started to get out of bed, then realized she was in her nightgown. "I'll talk to him first. Then he can talk to the police."

The men left the room to give Laura time to dress. Glenda brought her a skirt and sweater from the closet. "How are you holding up, Glenda? Did you and Kyle have the talk he promised?"

She shook her head. "We tried last night; then when Darren didn't come home . . . I keep hoping things will get better. But they just keep sinking worse and worse. Now Kyle will never have time for me. He's talking about taking Darren away, to give him a fresh start with new friends, get him in a school with accelerated classes and a good computer science program."

"Kyle would give up his practice here to help Darren?"

"He'll do anything. And I feel so selfish because I know he's right. Darren has too much potential to waste, but we have potential too—Kyle and me together. We could build something really great."

"I wish I could help."

"You are helping. Just listening helps. And here you are, getting out of your sickbed to go rescue the kid who put you there."

Laura laughed at the heroic image. "No, no. I'm feeling all right. And Darren didn't hit me."

On the way to the church, though, she wondered just how she did feel. Not merely physically. Her headache was barely perceptible—at a level she wouldn't bother taking an aspirin for. And she had no dizziness as long as she didn't move too suddenly. But what about her involvement in all this? Of course, she wanted to help her friends, and she felt a real affection for the bright, confused boy, caught midstep at his most appealing vulnerability between boy and man. Her heart went out to him as she thought of him hiding in some corner of a dark, cold stone cathedral. She knew the pain inside him was far worse than her headache, even at its sharpest.

But what about that other pain? The one in her heart. The one they had come to Victoria hoping to heal. Was it to the level that she no longer needed to take aspirin for it? There was no way to know until she and Tom could be alone to talk—and maybe more than talk. But at least Tom had said he wanted—needed, even—to talk to her. Even his saying that showed progress. Didn't it?

But first she had a job to do. She faced the massive gray stone building. Christ Church Cathedral was huge. Where would she find one small boy in there? Could she go in and call? Would he come to her? What if the door was locked?

As she stood contemplating, two women entered a side door carrying flowers. Must be the day for the altar guild. So much for the idea of going in and just calling Darren's name. He wouldn't show himself in front of other people. Tom had tried to insist on going in with her, but Kyle thought that would undermine the whole exercise.

And Laura agreed. The last thing they wanted to do was frighten the lad into going into deeper hiding. She followed the women into the church. The nave echoed as the door clanged shut behind her. In spite of the small group arranging flowers and dusting pews down front, the building seemed empty.

The whole enterprise suddenly struck her as silly. That note could have meant anything. And it couldn't have been meant just for her. Tom was right; they should have gone to the police. After all, they had Tiegs, so Darren was in no danger now. Not in danger from that thug, at least. But he was still in danger from his own turmoil.

Laura remembered her own feelings at that age, the pain from the harsh things that had been done to her, her reaction to her mother's austerity . . . Darren's situation was entirely different. And exactly the same.

She looked around. Would he be under one of the pews? In one of the side chapels? Why hadn't she thought to ask Kyle if the church had a crypt? What about a baptistery? There must be hundreds of nooks and crannies here. Which one would he choose?

Then she thought. *Hunchback of Notre Dame*, Glenda had said. Quasimodo lived in the bell tower. She turned to the small door in the back corner of the nave. It creaked as she opened it. Laura surveyed the narrow stairway before her. The pain at the back of her head reminded her that there were few things in the world she wanted to do less than climb a dark stairway to a tower where someone just might be waiting to hit her over the head again.

No, that was silly. That overactive imagination Tom was always accusing her of. But then, maybe it wasn't imagination. Maybe it was good sense. She forced her feet upward, stiff-legged, one step at a time. "Darren?" She tried calling out in a wavery voice.

Did she hear a soft scuffle above her head? She told herself it could be mice. But the thought wasn't comforting. "It's me. Laura." Her voice echoed.

Her feet scraped the stones, each wedge-shaped tread circling upward. Another sound that could be a whisper. Or the sound of wings. Were there bats in this tower? She resisted the impulse to throw her arms over her head. The stairs curved around the tower, getting narrower as they went up. Laura grasped the cold iron handrail and carefully placed her foot on each worn stone step.

The stairway wrapped around two more turns, then Laura stepped out on a bare wooden floor in a small square room. Enough light filtered through the slatted vents to leave no doubt that the space was empty. She turned around slowly, looking for candy bar wrappers or footprints in the dust—any possible clue.

Then she saw, in the dimmest corner, a wooden stairway, really just a ladder, leading to a trap door in the floor above. Well, she'd come this far. She wasn't backing down now. "Darren." The sound of her own voice made her jump. "I'm coming up. Don't be afraid. If you're there."

The plank was heavy. Laura pushed up on it. It was probably locked. They wouldn't want vandals or pranksters getting up here playing the bells at odd hours. She gave one more shove. The covering above her head yielded so suddenly she almost lost her balance. It slammed back onto the overhead flooring, raising a cloud of dust. Laura sneezed violently.

A hand reached down the yawning aperture to help her up. She ascended the last three steps and came out on the landing with a flourish. Then she stopped, blinking. "Who are you?"

A girl with long blond hair and wide, frightened eyes faced her on the other side of the opening.

Chapter 17

"Janelle is your girlfriend from Calgary?" Glenda asked as she handed around the Big Macs and fries.

Darren nodded, wolfing half of his sandwich in two bites. They'd been over all the ground once, but it was so hard to take it all in, it seemed they needed to ask every question twice.

"I just don't see why you couldn't have told me." Kyle's hamburger cooled, untouched.

"You would have made her go home."

"Not if what you tell me is true." Apparently the badgerings that Lewis, Janelle's older half-brother, had plagued her with as a child were turning to more sinister demands now that she was growing up. And her single-parent mother, who doted on her bright and shining son, would not take the girl's complaints seriously. Darren had given a rather cryptic account of the situation, and Janelle had said almost nothing. The whole matter would take months—maybe years—of talking and counseling. "You should have told me, Darren. There's no way I can help you with something I know nothing about."

"Help? You mean you'll help Janelle too?" Darren had explained that he had agreed to work for Tiegs to get money to help Janelle. Several of his acquaintances at school did such things routinely to make money to buy drugs. Darren had reluctantly agreed to talk to the police.

But that could wait until these poor starved waifs had

eaten their fill. And until the six of them had all their questions answered.

"Of course I'll help. What on earth did you think you were going to do, anyway?" Kyle's voice clearly showed the tug-of-war he felt between anger at Darren's behavior and anguish over his love for the boy.

"We were going to go away together." It was the first time Janelle had spoken.

"Away? Where?"

"I don't know. Vancouver, maybe. Someplace we could get jobs." She dropped her head and the straight blond hair covered her face like a veil. "I could lie about my age. I look older, and Darren said—"

"I said I could take care of her!" There was a fierceness about the boy/man that almost made one think he could do it.

"Darren." Kyle gripped his brother's shoulder. "Is Janelle pregnant?"

"No! It's not like that. I haven't touched her."

Janelle's shoulders started to shake. Glenda put her arms around her.

Laura looked at Tom. "I think we should leave them to sort this out as a family."

Tom stood and offered his hand to help her from the booth. "Right." Tom turned to Kyle. "So long. Thanks for everything." He stuck out his hand. "We'll keep in touch. I'm sorry we have to get back to Boise, but it's business. We'll leave depositions—or whatever they want—with the police."

Laura couldn't believe she heard correctly. She just meant go back to the hotel. Not turn their back on everything. "Tom, wait—" He hurried her from the restaurant.

A few minutes later Laura was once again ensconced in the big bed in their Empress suite. But she was far from relaxed. "Tom, we can't just run out on our friends like this."

Glenda was the first girlfriend she'd ever had. Classmates, writers' club associates, neighbors—but this was different. "We should stay for the hearing. We can help."

Tom's laugh was more of a snort. "If the all-wise Dr. Larsen can't take care of his own family, what do you suppose we could do?"

Laura's heart dropped. She had hoped—a tiny, forlorn hope, but a glimmer nonetheless—that she could still get Tom to agree to counseling if she could postpone their departure. "That's unfair, Tom. Kyle couldn't help anyone who wouldn't talk to him, even in his own family. You can't judge him for not having helped Janelle. He didn't even know she existed."

"Hmph."

She pressed her point. "We shouldn't have left them like that. We can't just go off and never see them again—" Tom started to reply, but she rushed on, "What will happen now? They won't lock Darren up, will they? They can't put him in jail like a hardened criminal—" her voice rose.

Tom turned to her sharply. "That's enough. You're working yourself into a state, and you're barely convalescent. Now listen: I don't know what they'll do about the runaway girl, but Darren will likely be released to Kyle's custody until his hearing. And it's a good thing if the kid does sweat over what he's done. He was involved in a very, very serious thing. Making it too easy for him now is the worst thing that could happen."

"Tom, he's just a boy. He doesn't have any parents. He needs love, concern, guidance . . ."

"Please. Spare me more of this psychological mumbo jumbo."

"But Darren—"

"Darren is a young hoodlum who has broken the law and

almost broke my wife's skull. And he needs to pay for his crimes."

"Tom! You're heartless. Besides, he didn't hit me."

"Laura, he was an accessory. They were all in it together. Oh, sure, if you'd been killed, the guy swinging the pipe would get first degree and your darling Darren might get off with second. But do you really think that matters?"

Laura shook her head, tears of weakness forming at the edges of her eyes. She just wanted all those people to be happy—Darren and Janelle, Kyle and Glenda, Kevin and Gwendolyn. She wanted happiness for them as much as she wanted it for herself and Tom. But she was too tired to argue. Tom would never understand how she felt. She leaned back against the pillows and closed her eyes in defeat.

She took the painkiller and a glass of water Tom held out to her. "Good," he said. "You sleep. You need it. We'll talk later. But we do need to talk. When you feel like it." Tom turned out the light and left the room.

Laura tried to protest. If Tom wanted to talk, she wanted to listen. But she couldn't fight through the weight of sleepiness to say so . . .

I sleep, but my heart waketh: it is the voice of my beloved that knocketh, saying, Open to me, my sister, my love, my dove, my undefiled: for my head is filled with dew, and my locks with the drops of the night.

Laura woke sometime near midnight remembering how endearing Tom had looked in the hospital. How different. Surely something really important had happened. She had said they needed a miracle. Maybe it had happened. And here she'd been too involved in Darren's problems even to listen to Tom. No wonder he was so sharp in his approach to the boy's situation last night.

She heard the clacking of Tom's computer keys through

the French doors even before she opened them. "Hi. Working late?" She grinned at him as he looked up.

He stood up, rubbing his eyes. "Oh, my goodness, how the time gets away. You look better."

She stretched luxuriously. "Mmm, nothing like a good nap. Want to talk?"

Tom followed her back into the bedroom and sat on the edge of the bed facing her. "So much has happened, and we've talked so little, I hardly know where to start . . ."

She cozied back into the covers, waiting for him to get past the preamble, waiting to hear the good news. She smiled softly. *The voice of my beloved! behold, he cometh leaping upon the mountains, skipping upon the hills.*

". . . and then Phil called . . ." Suddenly she focused on Tom's words. *Phil? That was business. In the middle of all this turmoil with everyone's future hanging in the balance—the last night of their honeymoon—Tom wants to talk about business?*

"It's a disaster, Laura. The whole Kansas City project has fallen apart. I offered to fly home, or fly to K.C. to try to pick up the pieces, but there aren't even any pieces left to pick up."

"What happened?"

Tom ran his fingers through his hair—an indication of how upset he was. Tom never ruffled his hair. "It's all my fault. Phil didn't say so—you know what a perfect gentleman he always is. But I was so anxious for the whole thing to go. I guess I pushed too hard. All those phone calls . . . I meant to be encouraging them, shoring everything up, but I scared them off. They've decided to go with a local developer—a more conventional plan. Not as good a deal, but there it is."

He sat for a moment, looking at his hands. "I just don't know what we'll do now. We had banked on this so heavily—literally—and put in months of work, even turned down some smaller clients. We usually have several projects going at once, but this one was so big . . . I guess we made the mistake of putting all our eggs in one basket . . ."

Laura's sleep-fuzzed mind followed along obediently, not really taking it in: Kansas City, the project that was to put them over the top, the project that had to have Marla's money. She sat up so abruptly she and Tom almost bumped heads. "Oh, Tom, that's wonderful!" *Kansas City? The deal off?* "Then you don't need Marla's money!" She lunged forward and threw her arms around him. "Now I understand what you're saying. I thought this was just business—that it didn't have anything to do with *us*. But you're telling me everything is great now!"

"Wonderful? Great?" He unwound her arms from his neck. "Don't you understand anything?"

"I understand this is a direct answer to prayer. The whole barrier to our happiness just crumbled like the Berlin Wall."

Tom gripped her shoulders. Hard. "Laura, the much-despised Marla's money is all that is keeping Marsden and James out of bankruptcy proceedings."

"OK. I'll take the bankruptcy."

Tom flung himself off the bed. "You may get your wish. Or you could take up mugging like your friend. Or go on the street with Janelle." He gave a sharp bark of laughter. "Ha. That would be an irony for Miss Frigidaire."

Laura put her hands to each side of her head. The pounding ache was back with a vengeance. "How can you say that? How can you be so heartless? So insensitive! You don't care about people at all. Not about Kyle and Glenda or Darren or—or me either. You're just a glorified, walking, talking, computerized bank statement! No wonder we haven't had sex for months. Here I thought it was all my fault. But no woman can make love to a—a machine!"

"Machine." His voice was cold, his eyes hard. "Is that what you think?" He grabbed her shoulders and pushed her down on the bed. "I'll show you just how this machine works."

Chapter 18

Laura moved stiffly around the room as the early streaks of sunrise glistened on the window. She would like to write in her journal. The incredible happenings of these past days should be recorded. But she felt a restlessness that wouldn't let her sit still long enough to write. She gently rubbed the back of her head. The swelling was almost gone now. Unless she did something silly like jumping up too fast, there was almost no pain. The pain was further down. Pain and a strange kind of ache that was mingled with longing. A homesickness that didn't have anything to do with going home.

Laura looked at her open suitcase, gaping like a hungry mouth. This was it. Their last day in Victoria. The last day of their failed honeymoon. She should be packing. They were going to make their final tourist stop at Fable Cottage, which was about halfway to the airport, then on to the latest flight out to connect with their Seattle-Boise plane. And that would be that.

The waters would close over all that had happened here. And they would struggle on as before. Well, not quite as before. But she'd already been over that ground, and it was a dead end. She didn't really want to think about what she was going home to. So she turned her thoughts to Gwendolyn and Kevin.

She couldn't stay in Victoria to help Glenda and Kyle, but she could bring about a happy ending for her fictional hero and heroine. At least she hoped she could. Sometimes fictional characters could be almost as difficult to maneuver as real people. They could take on a mind of their own and weren't about to be rushed—or to listen to her omnipotent advice. And in this case she was singularly devoid of advice anyway. She opened a drawer, pulled out a handful of lingerie, and plunked it in her case.

Tom yawned and stretched, then sat up with a big grin on his face and ran his hand through his hair. "Wow! What a good night of sleep. Must have been all that—" One could see the memory of the night before come on in his mind like a light in the room. He sank back against the headboard. "Oh, Laura. Last night. I'm sorry. I—I don't know what to say—"

Laura shook her head. "Don't apologize. A fight always takes two." She didn't want to talk about the fight. Or about what came after. Her thoughts were far too confused to verbalize, anyway. Still she wanted to talk. Talk about anything but last night. Tom, breathing hard, his hands sweaty like . . .

She dug around in her mind for some neutral ground they could discuss—something she could hold out as a kind of peace offering. Then she remembered. "Oh, I almost forgot. I saw something interesting the other day when I was driving around. Strange, really. There was this big housing development being dismantled."

"Dismantled?"

"Well, I don't know what you call it—like being put in cold storage or moth balls or something. Anyway, all these executive types were there closing the place down—hauling off tools and lumber, everything. I didn't know if you'd be interested or not, but I wrote down the telephone number . . ."

"Yeah, I might be interested." He glanced at the TV set. "I wonder when the local news is on. There might be something about it."

"I bought a newspaper yesterday—no, the day before. Or before that? I can't remember—" She looked around the room, frowning. Oh, there with the stuff she had dumped from her bag just before they discovered Darren's note. Somehow it seemed weeks ago.

It didn't take Tom long to locate the article on the real estate page—it was the top story complete with a photo. A major construction company in Victoria, which currently had three developments underway, had filed a bankruptcy petition the day before. All crews were being pulled off the sites and the projects were all going back to the bank. "This sounds great. Our plan is perfect for REO stuff, and banks hate to have Real Estate Owned property on their books. Where's that phone number?"

Laura listened to Tom's telephone conversations with one ear while she continued packing mechanically. He made his way through several bank officers, asking questions, giving brief explanations, and jotting figures on long yellow pads before he placed a call to Phil.

Apparently Phil wasn't in. Tom sat there, tapping his pen as he ran calculations in his head. "Shouldn't you be packing?" Laura finally asked. "We were going to stop at Fable Cottage, remember?"

Tom looked up from his figure-covered notepaper. Laura could read his mind as clearly as if it flashed in neon lights. He wanted to suggest she go on alone, and they'd meet at the airport. But second thoughts reminded him of her accusations last night. "Yeah, guess I'd better."

A very glum Laura sat on the floral Chippendale love seat, running the toe of her shoe over the pale green carpet and staring morosely at the useless fireplace. *Silly to have a fireplace that doesn't work—just makes you miss a crackling fire all the more. Just as silly as an unsuccessful honeymoon. Better not to have tried than to long for the crackling fire.*

Tom called for the bellboy. A minute later the phone rang. "Well, if they're too busy to carry our bags down, we'll do it ourselves." Tom strode toward the phone. "After all, we carried them up."

Yes, a lifetime ago that was, Laura thought. That bedraggled young woman who struggled into the room on that storm-tossed night with her arms full of suitcases and her head full of dreams—could that possibly have been her?

But the call wasn't from the bell captain. "Oh, hello, Phil. Thanks for returning my call—they said you wouldn't be in for the rest of the day . . ."

Laura moved to answer the knock at the door. The brown and beige uniformed man began loading their bags on his cart. Laura knew how long Tom's business calls could take, so she would go ahead and do the checkout routine.

"I hope you've enjoyed your stay with us." The clerk in a cheery tartan jacket pulled out Mr. and Mrs. James's paperwork.

"Yes. It was lovely." Then Laura looked across the lobby where the first sitting for early tea was being prepared. "But we never had tea here."

"Well, you must come back. Afternoon tea at the Empress is one of Victoria's most hallowed traditions."

"Yes, I know. We just never seemed to be able to work it in." It didn't really matter. There had been far more important things that they hadn't managed either. It didn't seem that anything much mattered now.

"If you'll just sign here, please." The lady held out the pen.

"Wait a minute. Don't sign anything yet." Tom pulled the pen from Laura's fingers and handed it back to the desk clerk. "We're staying. There's business to be done in Victoria."

"Tom! We don't have to leave?"

"No way. I've got an appointment with a vice president of First Provincial Bank over dinner this evening. But there's plenty of time to see that cottage thing this afternoon." Tom tipped the bellman and issued directions to have their luggage taken back upstairs, then ushered Laura out to the car.

With every step her spirits rose another level. *Reprieve, reprieve, reprieve,* was all she could think. One last chance to reach Tom. One free afternoon before it was back to business. And yet she held out little hope. She was too tired. She had tried too many times and failed. She didn't need another failure.

"Drop in on a Dream," Laura read the slogan of Fable Cottage and winced. She had spent much of the past few days seeing her dream slip through her fingers. She was no longer so sure about the value of holding to dreams. Yet when they traveled the wooded country lane, reminiscent of almost every English TV show she'd ever seen, and then at the end the blue, sun-sparkled waters of Cordova Bay spread out before them, Laura did sense the dreamlike quality of the place. "Look, even the doghouse has a thatched roof." How refreshing to see that—for some people at least—dreams did come true.

Their walk through Fantasy Forest took them past the private retreats of woodland dwarfs busy at whatever pleased them most. Gnomes frolicking on a water wheel beside a stream bank covered with clumps of mushrooms, begonias, and impatiens while bright blossoms floated in the water; child-sized elves harvested the rewards of a magical mine and emerging from the shaft on a jewel-laden cart; dwarfs fished at the old swimmin' hole. Laura smiled at the elf fishing in a leaky boat held afloat on the back of a giant green frog.

"Ribbit." Laura jerked around. Tom? Was it possible?

Once upon a time, a long time ago, Tom had mooed with cows, croaked with frogs, and chirped with birds. But she had lost hope that that once-upon-a-time Tom still lived. She was sure the little boy she loved had been strangled with a mathematical formula. Yet Tom had ribbited.

They entered the dream world together as the flowers that surrounded them in the pond and grew so riotously on the hills of the woods reflected their laughter. Here the viewer could be as childlike and carefree as the elves and gnomes who inhabited the place. Kyle had said something about the importance of keeping in touch with the child within oneself, but Laura had paid very little attention to the concept. Was this what he was talking about?

And then the light, freehearted voices of real children floated up the path. *What a wonderful place for children.* And with the thought Laura suddenly felt awkward and out of place. And a little guilty for taking up her adult-sized space in this world of childhood visions of innocence.

The next view, however, reminded them that there could be threats to peace even in an enchanted forest. The path rounded to the hut of the wicked witch with a Boarder Wanted sign in her garden. Yes, there could be dangers in living for a dream. But rewards too.

They went on to the top of the path and exited from Fantasy Forest. And there before them, at the far side of a rolling emerald lawn, the sun shining on its numerous, thatchedlike, high-pitched gables with eaves dipping almost to the ground, was the house that proved that even the real world could be built on dreams. There stood the real-life family home that had been built with dreams and love and imagination.

"Perhaps they were inspired by Anne Hathaway's cottage," Tom said.

"Yes, maybe. I can just hear them; the husband would say,

'I'd like to live in a house like that.' And his wife would say, 'Me too, but not Elizabethan. I'd rather live in a storybook—like every fairy tale I've ever read.' And the husband would be quiet for a bit and then say, 'Why not?' "

Just past a splashing fountain Laura stopped open-mouthed at the whimsical beauty of an enchanted tree, a flower with every variety and color of blossom imaginable. "Our favorite apple tree was dying, so we hung flowering baskets on it to brighten the days," the sign explained. A dead tree had been turned into a thing of fascinating beauty. It seemed that with love, vision, and humor any situation could be turned to good. *Hmm.* Laura boggled at her own thought.

They entered the barrel-shaped door, one of the hallmarks of the house, and were greeted by the guide. "It took 11 years to build the cottage, and the family lived here 10 years with their two children."

"Imagine how children must have loved living here." Laura self-consciously pulled her hand away from her abdomen.

The guide took them from room to room where the real-life family had lived in their fairy-tale surroundings: Under the arch of the walk-through fireplace, into a kitchen like the one Snow White must have longed for when she cooked for the Seven Dwarves, to the picture window in the living room with its view clear across the blue, blue bay to the San Juan Islands.

Laura ran her hand over the mirror surface of the red-gold wood of the coffee table, glistening in the light from the window. "I've never seen such a polish on furniture."

"The owner did that all himself," the guide said. "He made the furniture from our local yellow cedar and hand rubbed it with—I can't remember how many—coats of beeswax."

"It's all so wonderful. Why did they ever leave?"

"At that time the cottage was visible from the road, and sightseers just wouldn't leave them alone. At first they tried opening their home to tourists for a couple of months in the summer, but that still didn't satisfy the demand, so finally they sold it as a public attraction."

Laura walked from the house slowly. "What a shame they couldn't just live here and enjoy their dream."

"But some dreams have to be shared." Tom took her arm on the uneven path.

"What would Victoria be without its dreamers and their buildings?" Laura mused. "Just think, Butchart Gardens, the Old England Inn, Craigdarroch Castle, and now Fable Cottage—all were built as private residences."

"Yes." Tom grinned at her. "And would you believe—the Empress Hotel too?"

Laura giggled. "No, I wouldn't."

Arm in arm they strolled through the Wishing Gardens. Laura paused at the True Love wishing spot. "I like having gray-haired elves on lovers' lane. It means more than showing romantic youngsters."

"Love endures. 'There is no limit to its faith, its hope, and its endurance.' " *Tom* said that? What had happened to him? He seemed so different. That was one of the most romantic things he had ever said to her. She turned to him open-mouthed.

And when she turned he was already bending toward her.

All her wishes, hopes, and dreams were in that one kiss. Her wishes for their marriage to grow solid and strong—a fortress where their two spirits could flower and produce fruit; her hopes of building a family—a real family that nurtured and supported, yet allowed freedom for creativity; her yearnings to love Tom freely—physically.

She stood long in the curve of his arms, longing to go with her beloved into the wine garden . . .

My beloved spake and said unto me, Rise up, my love, my fair one, and come away. For, lo, the winter is past, the rain is over and gone; the flowers appear on the earth; the time of the singing of birds is come; and the voice of the turtle is heard in our land; the fig tree putteth forth her green figs, and the vines with the tender grape give a good smell.

"My love is beautiful." Tom's words were such an incredibly perfect continuation of the poetry in her head that it took Laura a moment to realize he had spoken.

And then his words flowered in her mind. Tom had called her beautiful—love. She wanted to answer him, but all she could do was make a choking sound and lean more tightly into his arms.

His touches on her neck were like drops of burning sunshine. "Tom—"

And then the sound of approaching voices required that they pull apart. "Now I understand why the owners sold this place," Tom muttered.

And then the old Tom looked at his watch. "Oops, I have to make a phone call." He pulled out his cell phone. "Do you want to wait here?"

"Yes, I'd like to stay here." Preferably forever. The trouble with dreams was waking up from them and finding they *were* dreams. But Tom was the realist, the businessman, the one who never forgot an appointment—because it would be illogical to do so. For once, though, Laura was amused rather than irritated by his methodical habits.

She sat on a bench facing a giant cornucopia spilling forth its floral blessings in mounds of copper chrysanthemums, silver astilbe, and golden marigolds. She smiled at the appropriateness of the monetary theme as Tom walked to the far side of the garden to place his business call.

Almost without conscious effort she opened her notebook. In this wonderful setting, fresh in the glow of a few moments of real tenderness with Tom, she wanted to write a poem, a song, a magnificat. That was it, she wanted to worship. *Glory be to the Creator and to the Son and to the Holy Ghost.* She paused, her pen suspended in midair. She knew the traditional words, "Glory be to the Father . . ." But she couldn't say that.

She shivered at the image of a Father God. She had heard the phrase often enough in church, but never in her own mind or heart. The idea of God as a father—someone close and intimate was—she sought for the word—repellent. She never even said the first line of the Lord's Prayer. She had never had a father. She had never needed one. And she could continue doing very well without one, thank you.

That settled, she turned back to the page waiting blank before her. *I want to worship You, Lord; I want to worship You, Christ; I want to worship You, Spirit. I want to love You, Lord; I want to love You, Christ; I want to love You, Spirit. I want to praise You, Lord; I want to praise You, Christ; I want to praise You, Spirit.*

She sighed at the trite expression and put the cap on her pen. Somehow her exercise hadn't produced the epiphany she had hoped for. Something was lacking, but she didn't see what it could be.

All the way back to town she sat close to Tom, concentrating on her dream. It could last. It could. With Tom's cooperation they could apply the new things she had learned—continue her progress. Physical and spiritual ecstasy could come together in their home. They would live in their garden always . . . *I went down into the garden . . . to see whether the vine flourished, and the pomegranates budded.*

But like Adam and Eve, the owners of Fable Cottage had been driven from their Eden. How long could she and Tom dwell in theirs?

Chapter 19

Laura rang the doorbell on Glenda's apartment in high spirits. After her fantasy afternoon with Tom, Laura looked forward to spending a cozy evening with her friend while Tom had his business meeting. Glenda had sounded so surprised and pleased when Laura called to explain that they were still in Victoria. "Yes, come over this evening. I should have news. I'm seeing Kyle in a few minutes."

"You're finally going to have that 'appointment'?"

"Yes, and you can't imagine how nervous I am."

"Don't worry. I'm sure it'll go fine."

Laura couldn't wait to hear the good news. She raised her hand to the bell again when the door flew from her reach. One look at her friend told Laura that desperation had replaced Glenda's earlier happiness. Glenda engulfed Laura in a hug. "Thank goodness you're here."

Glenda drew her from the doorway and onto the deep plush sofa. Words tumbled from Glenda as fast as she could move her mouth. "It's this awful mess with Darren. Kyle is determined to take him away if the judge will let him. He's talking about going to Toronto. I feel like I'll never see him again."

"And what about Janelle?"

"Kyle talked really straight to those kids. But I don't know if they listened. Kyle was adamant about calling Mrs. Wilson, Janelle's mother. I thought he and Darren were going to have a shouting match—or worse—right there in McDonald's. But

Kyle promised he wouldn't tell where Janelle was unless her mother agreed to listen to what she had to say about Lewis."

"And she agreed?"

"Well, Mrs. Wilson said she'd listen. But who knows. If Kyle isn't convinced she'll shelter Janelle from her half-brother, he'll petition to have her put in foster care."

Laura grimaced. "That sounds dreadful."

"Yeah. Well, we can hope for the best. Mrs. Wilson will be here tomorrow, and we'll see. Kyle has a thing or two to say to her."

Laura leaned forward with a jerk. "And I've got something to tell them too." Even as she said it, she realized she had never considered such a possibility before. She had kept her story hidden for so long, even denied it to herself as much as she could. It had never occurred to her that she might be able to tell it in a way to help others. If she spoke out, she might be able to make other parents listen to their kids better and react more honestly. She might be able to save others from going through much of the anguish she had known. It would be nice to help another. Yet she shrank from the thought.

Maybe in one of her stories—she could use the experience in developing a fictional character with safe anonymity. But to look another person in the face and speak about it . . .

"Oh," Laura suddenly realized Glenda was waiting while she daydreamed. "Sorry. Bad habit of mine. And what about Darren?"

"It's hard to tell. He seems to realize how unrealistic he was being—that Janelle needs to get things straightened out at home. And I think he understands how serious—and foolish—the things he was doing were."

"So it sounds like a new start is the right thing for him."

"Oh, yes." Glenda hit her hand into the sofa cushion. "I suppose I should be happy. Maybe I'm just being selfish. I certainly don't mean to be putting my happiness ahead of Darren's welfare. I just want there to be room for me too."

"I'm sure there will be. Things will work out. You'll see." The more Laura insisted, the more hollow her words sounded even to herself. The best she could do was promise that she and Tom would be at Darren's hearing.

Laura's head reeled as she returned along the street lined with white-globed Victorian lampposts cascading with baskets of flowers. When she got up this morning she thought she would be back in Boise unpacking by this time tonight. Back home with nothing changed.

Instead, here she was still in Victoria, and so much had changed. It was easy to shut out Glenda's problems as her mind drifted again to the floral-scented garden and she imagined herself in Tom's arms once more. Even in simply recalling the warmth she had felt all the tightly closed buds inside her beginning to uncurl.

Not bursting flowers yet, but small tips of color, showing the promise of bloom. And it was strange because so little had really changed. Tom was still Tom, dashing off to his business meeting. And—she made herself think it, even as she winced—Marla was still Marla, holding all the moneybags.

And yet Tom had expressed his love, and Laura had warmed to it. Surely Marla could be forgotten.

Laura slipped her key in the lock and stepped into her hotel room. Then jerked back. She had the wrong room. No, the key fit. It was the right number. But this room was alight with candles, a spicy vanilla fragrance floated on the air, and the soft strains of a Mozart aire came from the bedroom.

"Come wiz me to ze Caasba, my dahlink."

"Tom! You idiot! What is going on?" She looked around in amazement. "How did you manage a fire in the fireplace? I've been longing for one."

197

"Look again, my observant darling."

"Oh, candles!" Tiers of votives lined the artificial logs. "You're an absolute genius. I can't believe all this."

"Why don't you slip into something more, ah, comfortable, and I'll tell you all about it. We've needed to talk for days, but in case you hadn't noticed, it's been a bit hectic around here."

"Something more comfortable." At last Laura had a chance to wear the red caftan. While she was changing, room service arrived bearing a tray of after-dinner tea and an assortment of canapés and pastries. Honeymooners at last, Tom and Laura sat on the love seat in front of the fireplace sipping tea and feeding each other tasty tidbits while the candlelight danced warm and live around them.

Tom leaned back and regarded her for several moments. "You are beautiful."

Laura gave a small laugh and ducked her head. "I don't know what's come over you. But please don't stop. Every woman needs to hear those words—even if they aren't true. Maybe she needs it most when they aren't true."

"Laura?" Tom sat forward and held her by one shoulder. "What are you saying? Do you mean you don't believe you're beautiful?"

She ducked her head lower. "I know I'm not. But it's lovely to hear anyway."

Tom shook his head. "I can't believe this. Kyle must have been right."

"Right about what?"

"He said he had never counseled a sexually unresponsive woman that had a good self-image. I said that was ridiculous. You're so beautiful, so successful—you couldn't possibly have a poor self-image."

Laura stared at the sofa cushion, not daring to believe

what she heard, yet longing to.

Tom ran his hand up her arm, gliding over the sensual silkiness of her gown. "He said that professional success wouldn't build your sense of self-worth if you felt you were a failure in bed. You see, I always took it for granted that you knew—that reinforcement from your mirror and your readers was enough."

Laura shook her head, incapable of speech.

"Kyle said your mirror and your readers weren't your husband and that what you would really believe were the messages from me." Tom turned away. "That was pretty tough for me to swallow, because he was telling me that an enormous share of our problems were my fault. And all this time I'd been feeling so righteous because I was putting up with *your* problem."

Laura's voice came out in a jagged whisper. "I think a man should always tell the women he loves she's beautiful. It's another way of telling her she makes his life beautiful."

And then Tom was making her life beautiful with a kiss that spoke to her of beauty and affection far beyond anything mere words could say. This was a kiss she could keep forever in her heart—a kiss to hold fast, to savor, to cherish. Tom was giving her a gift of himself.

Even after they pulled apart they sat in the incandescence of the electricity that kiss had created. It was a glow to light their whole life with affection and caring.

At last Laura spoke. "And when did Kyle say all this to you?"

"That's what I've been wanting to tell you about. That afternoon you were out getting yourself bashed over the head I had an appointment with Kyle. He said some of the most amazingly simple things—things simple enough to change our whole life: 'pay attention to her, make your time together special, be sensitive to her feelings, develop an attitude of romance—court her.' "

"For a beginner you're doing an incredibly expert job." She leaned to him.

"Laura . . ." His lips were against her hair. "I was so frightened in the hospital that night. So scared I might not get to tell you—to show you. And then you were OK, and I could have my chance . . . Then last night . . . everything went all wrong. I'm terribly sorry about that. I want to make it up to you. I want to make all our last nights up to you."

"Yes. That's exactly what I want too. A second chance— or a third or fourth or however many times we've tried. But for this one to be different."

She thought they would go to bed then, but instead, Tom stood up, kissed the top of her head, and said, "Don't go away."

She was surprised the next moment to hear the water running in the bathroom. What a strange time for Tom to take a shower. But it was pleasant not to be rushed. After all, they had the whole night. A terribly wanton thought crossed her mind—what would Tom think if she joined him in the shower?

Before she could act on any such idea, however, Tom came back looking inordinately pleased with himself. "I've got something for you."

Wondering what in the world he could have for her in the bathroom, she went to him. The room welcomed her with a delightful herbal scent, and there was Tom's surprise—the wide, oversized tub was brimful of hot, Caribbean blue water, and floating on its surface was one perfect, white rose, immaculate in its bridal purity.

"Oh!" She turned to him in delight, but could say no more.

Tom gently lifted the caftan over her head and kissed her smooth white shoulders. "Enjoy." He turned and closed the door softly behind him, leaving her to luxuriate in her personal spa.

Taking the fat bath sponge and new bar of country English soap Tom had left on the edge of the tub for her, Laura rubbed her arms and neck with the silkiness of its lather, feeling like the bride of an Eastern potentate being prepared for her marriage bed. *Thou hast ravished my heart, my sister, my spouse! . . . How fair is thy love . . . how much better is thy love than wine! and the smell of thine ointments than all spices!*

Laura smiled softly, trying to convince herself this was really happening. Since the moment she entered their suite it had been as if she had crossed the threshold into a fantasy world. That Tom could have prepared this extravagant romance for her was unbelievable. She had never even written such a scene in a book. It was a world beyond her dreams, and she was living in it.

If this be a dream, but let me slumber on. Even as she reveled, she knew that fantasies came to an end, that one wakened from dreams. The harsh light of day would soon enough intrude itself. But tonight would be theirs.

She dried herself with a thick, peach towel, used just a light dusting of powder, and slipped into her ivory satin gown. When she emerged, soft and rosy from her bath, Tom, clad in a deep blue velour robe, was waiting for her.

He held his arms open for her, and she glided across the room to him . . .

But she never reached the shelter of his embrace. The telephone's shrill shattered their romantic seclusion like an alien invader from a distant star.

It's too soon, Laura protested. She knew the light of day was coming. But surely not yet.

"Hello . . . Yes . . . Phil told you about the new deal? . . ."

Laura stopped breathing. Not even a flickering eyelash interrupted her concentration on Tom's words.

". . . Of course. I thought you'd want to invest . . . Very successful—it looks like a go . . . Sure, I've got the figures right here . . ." He snapped on the desk lamp, obliterating the final shreds of the atmosphere he had so carefully created. ". . . project A has 20 single-family homes and 60 town-houses, at a market value of—"

Laura shivered and realized the room had chilled as the candles flickered and died. She turned to go up the steps to the bedroom alone. She would wait for Tom there.

She was momentarily warmed anew by the sight that met her: The coverlet turned down, the sheet folded back, and on her pillow—a single, long-stemmed red rose. She twirled it between her fingers, smelling it absently. Red rose for true love. She didn't really doubt it. Tom loved her. Truly. His love for her came right after his passion for developing invest-ments. Marla's investments.

She slipped between the sheets, still holding the rose. And still listening to the statistical conversation from the next room . . . The room around her began melting like the wax on the candles, Tom's voice grew distant and furry . . .

She jerked awake. She *would* wait for him. Tom's words broke and floated away . . . Helplessly she glided back, as if her body were weighted.

Once again she fought her way up to the surface. But this time the candles were all guttered and the rose wilted.

Chapter 20

Tom came to bed sometime during the night. Laura knew because when she rolled over once her hand brushed his back. She quickly rolled as far as she could to her side of the bed. She wakened again when he got up in the morning, but she lay with her eyes tightly closed. It seemed like hours before she heard the lock on the hall door click shut as Tom left.

She considered calling room service for breakfast, but even a pot of tea sounded disgusting. Thank goodness she had one escape that never failed. Wrapping the hotel-provided terry cloth robe around herself she pulled out her laptop computer. Kyle and Glenda seemed caught in a hopeless situation, her own romance had smashed on the rocks of high finance, but there was one love story she could control:

At last the day arrived. The day Gwendolyn had feared would never come. She twirled in front of her mirror, admiring the turn-of-the-century lines of the ivory muslin and handmade lace of her grandmother's wedding gown. Lanette, her matron of honor, came in and helped her adjust the tulle trim on her wide-brimmed straw hat.

"Come on, Gwen, the guests are all seated. The chamber group has finished the Water Music, the Trumpet Voluntary is next." Lanette led her from the house to the hedge behind the rose garden and delivered the radiant bride to the arm of Ted, who was to give her away.

As the contrapuntal chords of the baroque masterpiece played at royal weddings since the days of Charles II filled the air, a lump rose in Gwen's throat, causing her eyes to mist with joy. On the other side of that hedge, at the end of the rose-strewn garden path, Kevin was waiting for her. Waiting for her as she had waited for him all her life. She lifted her face and smiled, hoping her smile would reach him as a kiss.

She matched her step to the lyrical, yet solemn music, and every step took her closer to her beloved. The scent of the rose trees lining the way came to her as an invocation—entreating their future happiness, and as a benediction—bestowing a blessing on their life together.

Kevin stepped forward.

As their hands touched she looked into his eyes and said yes to their whole future.

Laura looked around the room, dazed, with a sense of jetlag. It was so satisfying when the scenes would come like that—as fully developed pictures in her mind. She read back through her last chapter. Something had happened to her writing. It had always been adequate, but maybe a little stiff. Now it was singing.

Funny, all she had worked through in the past weeks with Tom might have fallen short of her goal to reach Tom, but at least it was having an effect on her creativity. Maybe if that aspect of her life was changing, she would eventually see more concrete changes. But it was hard to keep hoping. If last night had failed, she couldn't imagine anything that would produce success.

And she could think of nothing else either of them could do. Of course, Kyle had said it would take time, had counseled continued therapy, but how much good would more of the same do? She had thought that Tom's accepting help would be the key. But that last hope had failed too. And not for lack of trying.

Laura glanced at her hand holding the manuscript pages.

Then blinked to be sure it was her own. Fingernails. Almost. She had never grown fingernails in her life. But now each finger ended with a tiny white rim. Not enough to require filing, certainly. But someday . . . When was the last time she had chewed them?

New life. A sign of new life right at her fingertips.

She jumped when the door opened. "Ready for tea? Just time to make our reservations." Tom could have been asking the bank teller about their business hours.

Was it a grasping at hope, mere force of habit, or the fact that she was starving that made her jump up and rush to her closet? "It seems so early."

"Yes, we asked for first sitting, remember. But then, I never knew you to turn down tea."

"Certainly not now." She emerged in her uniform—skirt, turtleneck, and blazer. "My stomach was in a decidedly bad mood over something this morning, but I'm starving now."

"Nervous over the hearing, were you?"

"I guess so." It was easiest to agree. Actually she had forgotten all about the hearing. And the idea of talking to Janelle's mother. The thought of having to talk about Mr. Sanders—and her mother's denial, which had put her into almost 20 years of stifling denial . . .

"Watch out." Tom took her arm just in time to prevent her collision with a white-jacketed waiter. Tom guided her across the well-mannered lobby where they were seated in over-stuffed chairs with a small round table between them.

Laura leaned back and looked up at the ornate ceiling supported by ionic columns and hung with scrolled brass Edwardian chandeliers. She sighed. Maybe this atmosphere that never lost touch with its era of romantic elegance and gracious living would help her sort things out. Maybe here, with Tom beside her, she could think what else—if anything—

they could attempt to make this the honeymoon they had set out seeking. Professional counseling had done much: Laura had broken through her long-standing denial, grieved over her losses with her mother, sought new paths with Tom. And Tom had tried to do his part. That almost made it worse. Such an all-out attempt as last night's having failed left one thinking, "If that wouldn't work, what would?"

The waiter placed tiny round salvers before them and removed the little domed covers to reveal spongy English crumpets, steeped in honey and aswim in butter. In spite of using her fork, Laura still wound up licking her fingers.

And then her thoughts turned inward again. They had even worshiped together. Everyone said that was important. It had once been important in their lives, an importance she would like to recapture. But that, too, had come to nothing.

And now she had this unlikely notion that there might be some therapy in trying to help Janelle . . .

A waitress placed footed silver dishes of fruit salad and a selection of finger sandwiches before them. Laura looked up and saw Tom regarding her. Uh-ho, she knew how he hated it when she went off on her own thoughts. She scrambled around in her mental notes. Then surprised herself with a giggle. "Oh, I just remembered—I read the other day that when streaking was in vogue the Empress lobby came in for its share, but the streakers had the good taste to wear neckties."

Tom responded. "I heard one too. Seems there was a holdup attempt in the Garden Café. The cashier informed the miscreant that 'this sort of thing is not done at the Empress.' The gunman fired a shot into the ceiling and left."

"Oh, I love it! I wonder if I could use that in my story somewhere?"

"I thought you finished."

"Just the rough draft—an outline, some key scenes sketched—there's months of work yet. But the hardest part is over." She wished she could believe that about her other goals.

"Happy ending?"

"I hope so." *No, Tom means the book, stupid.* "Oh, I mean, of course. Whoever heard of a romance with an unhappy ending?"

"Romeo and Juliet?"

Laura laughed and refilled their cups with Empress Blend Afternoon tea while the waitress served homemade scones with thick Jersey cream and strawberry jam. "You win. But somehow I don't think drinking poison in a crypt would go over too well with my readers."

The silence that fell between them became ominous. Was Tom, too, wondering if their own romance would end in similar tragedy?

A tray of pink and white cakes sat before them untouched as Laura watched two elderly ladies at a nearby table rise to leave. Laura was reminded of the little dollar dowagers, coming down from their garrets, but ordering only hot water with which they brewed their own, cheaper, tea bags. Would her life be equally empty without Tom? Would she have anything more significant to live for than an afternoon ritual?

She had to keep fighting for Tom. She couldn't give up until every possible avenue had been explored. And they had come so close last night. Or had they? How much did Tom really care if a telephone call could wipe it all from his mind? Or was it not so much the call as the caller? Was it, as she suspected, *that woman?*

Fear of Marla gripped her, so she leaned forward and clasped her jacket around her—a gesture she hadn't used for weeks. What was Marla's power over Tom? Was it romantic or financial? Could Tom separate the two?

If Marla would stay put in the business office, Laura might be able to cope—forget her most of the time, accept her when memory intruded. But when she insisted on forcing herself on their honeymoon, it was simply more than Laura could handle.

"Are you ready? We don't want to be late for the hearing." Laura blinked at Tom's words, then forced herself to stand, shoulders back, head up, and walk from the room.

They gave their names to the bailiff at the courtroom door as juvenile proceedings were closed to all but those involved in the case. This would be somewhat informal, as it was just a preliminary hearing, not a full trial. Still, the judge presided with solemn dignity, emphasized by his mane of gray hair and heavy eyebrows. Darren sat at a table to the left with his counselor. Laura slipped into a seat next to Glenda, Tom beside her. "How's it going?" she whispered to Glenda.

"The judge is very thorough. He's going into every detail."

"How are you?"

Glenda shook her head. "I'll be glad when it's over. I just want the best—for everybody. But I don't know what that is."

The judge dismissed Sgt. Monaghan, who gave Laura a shy smile as he walked past her. Next Janelle was asked to step forward. She gave a rather muddled account of her running away to her old boyfriend and of Darren's attempts to take care of her. "He did it to help me," was her one theme. "He cares about me. He believes me."

Janelle's mother jumped to her feet in the back of the room—a buxom woman with blond hair that had once probably been natural. "That's not fair. I cared too. I was a good mother. It's not easy—raising two kids alone. I did my best."

Janelle tossed her long hair. "You never listened to me. You wouldn't believe me."

"No, I wouldn't listen to smutty stories. Why should I?"

Laura couldn't believe what she was hearing. Janelle could have been herself a few years ago. Or Mrs. Wilson could be her a few years hence. This had to stop. "Your Honor, could I say something?" Laura spoke without weighing the consequences.

The judge asked her to come forward and identify herself. She spelled her name for the court reporter and swore to tell the truth. Suddenly she had the floor. Now, what would she say? She was under oath to tell the truth. But what *was* the truth? She could tell the details of her experience—let it all hang out as people were so fond of doing on popular TV talk shows. But telling all wasn't the point.

Feeling as if she were talking to her mirror, she turned to Janelle. "Don't let this happen to you." Her gaze took in the mother too. "Don't do what my mother and I did. Don't lose each other."

She took a step toward Janelle. "Talk to your mother. Talk and talk and talk."

Janelle's gaze was directed toward Laura's shoes. "I tried. She won't listen. She doesn't believe me. She doesn't care."

"That's not true!" The cry from the back of the room was answered by the judge's gavel.

"Order, or I'll have the bailiff clear the room."

But Laura continued to the girl, "Then make her listen. Make her believe you. Keep talking. Don't run away from your problems—you can't." She paused to look inside herself. "I learned that—the hard way. Your problems follow you and get bigger and bigger. You have to face them and defeat them before they overwhelm you."

Laura hadn't planned to get so personal, but now she could see that her story was an important part of the picture. "I know what I'm talking about, Janelle. I was molested when

I was younger than you. My mother wouldn't believe me. So I just stuffed the pain down and tried to act as if nothing had ever happened. It doesn't work. You have to deal with it.

"If I hadn't, and if I should ever have a daughter, I would have treated her just like my mother treated me. And then my daughter would treat her daughter that way. Don't you see? It has to stop. You have to say, 'The past ends here, right now.' Get rid of the past so you can live for the future."

Laura was trembling so hard she barely made it back to her seat. She had very little idea what she had said. Her heart was pounding in her ears until she couldn't hear her own words on the last. The judge said something about this not being Janelle's hearing but that when hers came up he would look into ordering a guardian for her and counseling for her and her mother.

Laura closed her eyes. She had done it. She had actually pulled the whole thing out in public. And perhaps she had helped Janelle. The judge's words sounded hopeful. But what of her and Tom? She had hoped it would help them as well as Janelle and her mother. But if anything Tom seemed more withdrawn. He still sat beside her. Yet the emotional distance was miles. How many more failures could they survive?

Then the focus shifted to Darren. His lawyer reviewed the boy's record, placing heavy emphasis on Darren's high scores on academic ability tests and on his solid background. Then the judge questioned Darren: his participation in the mugging, his willingness to develop his intellectual potential, his goals for the future.

Laura couldn't help being proud of Darren. Well-groomed in sports jacket and sweater vest he looked far more like Kyle than she had realized—or he would, when his facial bones strengthened. The boy spoke well to the judge, not looking at the floor and muttering, but head up, eyes straight

210

forward, giving open answers in a clear voice—far different from the day he had lied his way into her company. And his attitude was commendable. He seemed truly penitent for what he had done, determined to start over and travel a better road this time.

Kyle presented his request that his brother be bound over to his custody. He briefly outlined his plan for moving to Toronto with the boy and placing him in a top private school where he could receive an accelerated academic challenge and develop his interest in computer science.

The courtroom was silent as the judge reviewed the notes in front of him. Laura held her breath. This boy's future hung in the balance, as did the future of her friends. Kyle's plan sounded good for Darren. But was it good for Glenda and Kyle? If Kyle sacrificed his own happiness for his brother's, would it be good for Darren in the long run? And what of all the patients Kyle would be leaving?

Then all other questions fled from her mind as Tom stood up. "If it please the court, I would like to present an alternate proposal for consideration—"

Laura couldn't believe her ears. Tom offered to accept custody of Darren. *Tom.* What did this mean? She had to admit the idea didn't sound quite so wild as Tom outlined the excellent Advanced Placement Program offered at Boise High, the computer science courses available through the local university, the opportunity of a part-time job in Tom's office . . .

Darren? Living in their home? What would that factor do to their shaky marriage? What would that mean to her? Extra laundry and cooking, meeting the demands of another schedule, another human being . . .

But over and above all, the astounding thought of Tom in the role of a father. She could see herself as a mother. But a *father.* She would be living with a father. The idea stunned her.

She didn't even have uncles or male cousins, let alone a father. The only man she had ever been close to other than Tom was Mr. Sanders. She shivered.

People prated on and on about God being our father, but that was never a concept to which she could bear to give any consideration.

And now Tom as a father? Of course, if they'd ever had children of their own she would have had to face this, but she vaguely assumed that would be different.

Suddenly she realized the courtroom was silent. Everyone was looking at her. "I said, what do you think of this proposal, Mrs. James?" The judge looked at her from under his bushy eyebrows.

"I—"

"Can I speak?" Darren's question saved her. "Thank you, sir. Thank you very much." He gave Tom a wide, amazed grin. "Thank you. Er—, that is, that's a great offer. And I promise you I'll work very hard to justify your faith in me." He turned back to the judge. "But couldn't I stay here and just study harder? That is—I was listening to everything Mrs. James said about not running away. Going to Boise would be running away, wouldn't it?"

He turned to Kyle. "And so would going to Toronto. I mean, it's absolutely fantastic that you would move all that way just to give me a fresh start, but—" He looked at the floor. "Couldn't we stay here—and be a family—with Glenda, too, that is?"

Somehow the judge managed to wind up the hearing with sufficient order to preserve the proprieties of the judicial system. Among other procedures he outlined the probationary period Darren would serve under strict supervision.

But Kyle's talking about going down the hall to the marriage license bureau and Glenda's chatter about a garden wedding seemed to be primary among the topics of conversation that whirled around Laura as she struggled to sort out her feelings.

Tom had done a beautiful, generous thing. The Tom she had accused of being nothing more than a cold, calculating business machine cared enough for this boy to volunteer to take on a father's responsibilities for him. She was the one who had pulled back. She still didn't know what she would have said if Darren hadn't intervened. But her head was aching far too insistently to allow coming to any insights now.

"You look done in, Laura. You need some rest." Tom led her from the buzzing room and drove back to the hotel.

Each step made a jarring throb as they walked across the pomegranate red hall carpet to their room. Tom held the door for her. She walked in.

"Surprise!"

A woman with strawberry blond hair and long, sexy legs walked across the room toward them. What was *she* doing in their hotel room? "Sorry about invading your hideaway, but the maid was most helpful when I gave her a tearful story about a family emergency. She understood that I couldn't possibly wait out in the hall under such devastating circumstances."

"Marla!" Tom strode across the room to the intruder. But Laura couldn't move.

"Surprised to see me?" Her smiled seemed confident of welcome. "Phil and I spent hours going over all those figures you gave me last night. Then I went straight to the airport. There isn't a minute to lose on this deal. But I'm absolutely starved. And we don't want to bore Laura with our talk. Why don't we go over this at dinner?"

Laura didn't realize Tom had turned back to her until she felt his hand on her arm drawing her into the room. "Laura, I have to deal with this. I'll try not to be too late."

The next thing Laura knew she was alone in the room. Alone in the cold and the dark. It didn't even occur to her to seek a chair until her legs got so tired she simply sank down on the carpet. She felt no pain or anger. She only vaguely understood that Marla had come. And Tom had gone with her.

Part of the time Laura thought she was home in Boise in her favorite chair, writing in her journal . . . she had walked into Tom's office and found Marla in his arms. Then she was in a hotel room, huddled on something soft, but she couldn't write because it was too dark . . . and Tom wasn't there to turn on the lights for her.

Tom wasn't here. He was with Marla. And there were no lights.

Chapter 21

A wave of nausea brought Laura out of her paralysis. It was still dark, not the earlier darkness of emotional blindness, but the normal darkness of night—a night in which no lights shone. A second wave of sickness forced her to grope her way to the bathroom.

When the violence had spent itself, she made her way to the shelter of the bed. Even with keeping the quilted bedspread on for warmth, however, she was unable to dispel the chill that held her. Had she picked up some virus? Or was this a complication from having been hit on the head? The hospital had been so thorough, an MRI after the X ray, surely they hadn't missed anything. But she had been feeling strange lately. Was it possible for brain damage to show up this much later?

She wondered if the Empress kept a house physician, but she didn't have the energy to go to the phone. She just lay there in her black, icy cocoon, too weak even to shiver.

She felt she might have simply lain there until the end of time, but hours later another attack of queasiness drew her out of bed. A glance at herself in the mirror decided her on one thing: if she was going to die she had no intention of doing it alone in a hotel room—while her husband was out with another woman.

She dialed the front desk and asked them to call her a taxi.

"Royal Jubilee Hospital, emergency room, ma'am." The driver's voice penetrated her misery.

Some time later Laura was back in another taxi, feeling even more benumbed than before. She just couldn't take in the full implications of the doctor's report. At least she wasn't dying. But if she got back to the hotel and Tom was still out with Marla she might prefer to be. Could she cope without Tom? Could she cope *with* Tom?

She approached their room slowly. Would Tom be waiting with open arms and a believable excuse for having been gone all night? Or would he be there to tell her it was over? That Marla had won? Or would she just find the same cold emptiness she had left? Which would it be, the lady or the tiger?

Being met by a snarling tiger would have been preferable to the void she walked into. Before, the room had been merely empty. Now it was deserted. A body from which the soul had departed. A destitute shell.

She stood in the middle of the floor, trying to figure out what had changed. Why was the room so much emptier, colder, than when she left? The papers were still scattered around her computer on the side table, the bedcovers still rumpled in the room beyond, the books still on the coffee table, Tom's papers . . . That was it.

Tom's things were gone.

She opened the closet. Tom's clothes were gone.

Tom was gone.

Like a wounded animal she crept to the bed and curled herself into a ball. She longed to be able to cry. Or to scream. But the emotional toll of the past weeks had been too great. She had spent all she had of grief and joy, of pain and hope. Now there was nothing.

Nothing.

No, there was something. She was alive. There was life in the universe. She could reach for that life.

Without conscious thought Laura took the path up the hill

that she and Tom had taken on that bright Sunday morning that now felt so long ago—her glowing hopes for that morning now seeming so naive. And later she had returned in an equally dewy-eyed effort to rescue Darren from himself. Now she needed sanctuary. She needed someone to rescue her from herself.

Today there were no altar guild ladies fussing with flowers, only the marvelously radiant light through the jeweled windows. No robed priest served Communion today, but Laura knelt at the altar anyway, looking upward, seeking focus. The stained-glass Christ opened His arms to her. He was her priest. And she opened her heart to Him. The quiet beauty of hushed holiness flooded her soul.

She had no idea how long she knelt there, silent, but not alone, reveling in the warmth, the joy, the peace . . . At last she moved to pick up a prayer book. It opened at the familiar words, "Our Father who art in heaven . . ."

Laura pulled back. Those words. Intruding in her rapture. That unspeakable word—Father. God as Father; Tom as father. Her gaze turned to the window in the side chapel. Pretty, the blend of colors and figures . . . suddenly she jerked upright. The figure in the white robe with his arms spread out to the tattered, suppliant. She knew that story. Some long-forgotten Sunday School teacher had told the story of the prodigal son—and the father who welcomed him with open arms. The father who didn't just accept a penitent, but actually sought him with outgoing love. Was that the father she had always rejected?

Could she accept Him now—or really, let Him accept her? If she found harmony with God as Father, could she find like accord with Tom?

The prayer book fell from her lap with a thud. She picked it up and turned the pages, still trying to sort out all the new thoughts flooding her mind. Her eyes read the words before her mind took them in. "The union of husband and wife in heart, body and mind is intended by God for their mutual joy; for the help and comfort given one another in prosperity and adversity; and, when it is God's will, for the procreation of children and their nurture in the knowledge and love of the Lord."

Was that what Kyle had meant when he said something about marriage being a sacrament? Laura didn't know much about theology, but they were beautiful words. It was a beautiful, might-have-been idea. *The Book of Common Prayer* made a better fairy-tale book than Hans Christian Andersen. "Most gracious God, we give you thanks for your tender love in sending Jesus Christ to come among us . . . for consecrating the union of man and woman in his name . . . pour out the abundance of your blessing upon this man and this woman . . . Let their love for each other be a seal upon their hearts, a mantle about their shoulders, and a crown upon their foreheads . . ."

Why did she see it only now? Now that it was too late?

She paused at the back to light a candle for Tom. Wherever he was. Whatever he was doing. The flame rose golden and bright, glowing in its small red glass.

Chapter 22

. . . and so there it is. I put our marriage first. Tom put the business first. We were both wrong. Everything was in the wrong order. Something—Someone—else had to come first. I used my work to shut out everything else just as much as Tom did.

A story—I remember a story—young women invited to a wedding. Silly, careless girls who let their lamps burn out. And so they missed the feast. The wedding feast.

I am one of those silly creatures. I let my oil run out. My flame died. And now I see my mistake. Too late.

Tom gone off with Marla. And I'm here in a dark world with an empty lamp. Oh, Tom, are you sure she'll make you happy?

Laura's pen stilled as she stared at the door. If only she could have another chance. If only she could see Tom walk through that door just once more. She turned back to her journal, but no words would come. Only the deep, deep sadness of regret. *Too late, too late.*

The maid rattled the door, but Laura didn't look up. Housekeeping had already been there, they—"Tom!"

He stood before her like something conjured from her deepest longing with his arms full of roses. Were they for Marla? Why had he brought them here? "Laura, thank God you're here."

"Where did you think I'd be?"

"I didn't know. When I came back you were gone—out for an early breakfast, I guessed—but you were gone so long. I made all the arrangements, then I began to worry."

"Arrangements?"

"Oh." He looked at the roses as if he'd forgotten he was carrying them. "Roses for my bride." He placed them in her arms. "I've come to carry you off to a real honeymoon. All we have to do is gather up your stuff—I already put mine in the car."

Tom's luggage was in the car? Waiting for her?

Laura's journal slipped to the floor. Tom bent to pick it up. "Read it," she said.

His eyes skimmed the page, then he dropped to his knees beside her. "Oh, Laura, you thought . . . of course you did. I see how it looked." He struck his head with his palm. "Stupid. I should have left you a note. But I wanted to surprise you. And I thought I'd be back in a few minutes—but then it took me forever to find a florist, and all the traffic—"

He took her hands. "Laura, I'm so sorry. I shouldn't have marched Marla off like that without explaining to you. But all I could think of was getting rid of her—getting her away where she couldn't hurt you anymore. I didn't have any idea it would take so long—negotiating all the business. But I wanted it settled. Final."

"What settled?"

"The business. I wanted Marla out of our lives. Every aspect of our lives. No amount of money is more important than our marriage. The financial concerns got in the way of everything—friends, you, God. Laura, can you forgive me for putting you through so much?"

She looked at the dew-fresh roses nestled in her arm. "Well, you never promised me a rose garden." She grinned. "I wonder if Jenny ever said that to Mr. Butchart?" And then her practical side surfaced. "But what about the business? Where will you get the money?"

"I think I can get the bank here to finance it. But, anyway, these projects—which you found, my darling—" he paused to kiss the tip of her nose, "are such good ones, we'll make it."

Laura grinned. "Do I get a finder's fee from the deal?"

"You get the dealer. If you still want him."

She dropped her bridal bouquet and opened her arms to her bridegroom. *My soul shall be joyful in my God; for he hath clothed me with the garments of salvation, he hath covered me with the robe of righteousness, as a bridegroom decketh himself with ornaments, and as a bride adorneth herself with her jewels.*

Tom pulled back and lifted her to her feet. "Shall we go?"

"Go?"

"That's my surprise—our honeymoon at the Old England Inn. I can't wait to get started on it."

As they drove toward their new life Laura realized she was alone in the car with Tom. Truly alone. Marla was no longer there sitting between them. And now she could even feel sorry for Marla. How desperately unhappy she must be to throw herself at a man like that. All she had was her money and her surface beauty. Perhaps in time Laura could even come to pray for her.

The inn welcomed them with its wonderful Tudor timelessness. Laura stood in the grand entry hall and looked around her. "Stepping back in history—"

"In order to step forward into the future—our future." Tom swept her off her feet and carried her up the wide, red-carpeted stairway. But at the top he let her walk again. "Don't want to use all my strength on heroics." He grinned.

Laura's heart turned over. There was the boyish grin she had married and thought gone forever. The afternoon sun shone through the beveled and leaded windowpanes, engulfing them. *Let their love for each other be a seal upon their hearts, a mantle about their shoulders, and a crown upon their foreheads.*

Tom led the way down a narrow, crooked hallway to the golden heart marking the honeymoon suite and into the rich, red velvet draping of the Elizabethan room.

While the liveried footman brought up their luggage, Laura pulled an arrangement of dried flowers out of a vase and filled it with water for her bouquet. She placed the roses on an aged black oak chest, then noticed the carving. "Oh, Tom, come look!" She couldn't believe what she was reading. " 'IH & GH 1660.' This was a wedding chest—remember when the guide at Anne Hathaway's cottage told us about them? A groom carved this for his bride in the year Charles II was restored to the throne." She ran her fingers over the raised letters and Tudor roses. "Just think of it!"

"I am thinking." There it was—that wonderful grin again. "The chest is great, but there's another piece of furniture in here that interests me more." He drew her over to the massive black oak bed with its deep velvet curtains trimmed in gold braid and pulled her to the fur spread. "My beloved, my bride, my wife." He lay beside her.

"Yes, all that." She smiled softly. "And I'm something else too. I'm also the mother of your child. At least I will be in just under nine months. I saw a doctor this morning."

"Laura . . ." He choked. "There really aren't enough ways to say thank you, are there?"

"No, but this comes close." She reached over to the nightstand for the Bible there. "By night on my bed I sought him whom my soul loveth: I sought him, but I found him not . . . But I found him whom my soul loveth: I held him, and would not let him go."

Tom took the book from her hand. "Thou art beautiful, O my love. How beautiful . . . Thou hast ravished my heart, my sister, my spouse; thou hast ravished my heart . . . A garden inclosed is my sister, my spouse; a spring shut up, a fountain sealed."

But the springs, no longer shut up, were bubbling inside Laura. The fountain would never again be sealed against her husband. "The fountain in my garden is a spring of running water, 'a fountain of gardens, a well of living waters, and streams from Lebanon. Let my beloved come into his garden, and eat his pleasant fruits.' "

The book slid from her hand as she became increasingly aware of her husband's touch. As the minutes melted and their experience deepened, Laura became aware of a subtle change. The significance shifted from physical intimacy to spiritual intimacy, as if the closer she came to Tom, the closer she came to God. Giving unselfishly of themselves, they were no longer isolated individuals, but a perfect whole. Truly one—one in each other and one in Christ. The joyous communion between them became a channel for intimacy with the Father.

Like Adam and Eve before the Fall, they stood in the presence of God, the God that had created them for love. Tom's voice came to her softly, "I have come to my garden, my beloved, my bride, and have plucked my myrrh with my spices; I have eaten my honey and my syrup, I have drunk my wine and my milk."

References and Acknowledgments

The Book of Common Prayer (London: Eyre and Spottiswoode Ltd., 1964).

Gallagher, C. A., G. A. Maloney, et. al., *Embodied in Love, Sacramental Spirituality and Sexual Intimacy* (New York: Crossroad Publishing Company, 1983).

Heggen, Carolyn Holderread, "Working Toward a Theology of Sexuality," *Herald of Holiness*, July 1997, 20–31.

LaHaye, Tim and Beverly, *The Act of Marriage: The Beauty of Sexual Love* (Grand Rapids: Zondervan, 1976).

Peters, Jim, "The Other Woman," *Herald of Holiness*, November 1997, 21–23.

Schalesky, Marlo, "Cross-Gender Friendships: Are They Dangerous to Your Marriage?" *Herald of Holiness*, November 1997, 24–35.

Thank you, Bob Mack, Detective, Violent Crimes Division, Boise Police Department.